FRANK RYAN

Frank Ryan is a distinguished author who has written a "Book of the Year" for *The New York Times* and another that was the "Chosen Book" for Charlie Munger. His books have been acclaimed worldwide and translated into many languages.

He is a graduate of Sheffield University, to which he is still affiliated, and lives in South Yorkshire.

Also in fiction by Frank Ryan

The Doomsday Genie
Goodbye Baby Blue
Sweet Summer
Tiger Tiger

Between Clouds and the Sea

Acknowledgements

I'd like to thank my wife Barbara, my son John and daughter Catherine for their invaluable assistance in writing this book. I am also indebted to Norman and Val and Derek and Christine, for their help and advice, not to forget Duncan – my profound thanks to you all. Finally I should acknowledge the generous assistance of the Imperial War Museum, who generously allowed me access to their files, particularly those related to the Normandy landings.

Between Clouds
And the Sea

Frank Ryan

SWIFT
PUBLISHERS

SWIFT PUBLISHERS

First published in e-format 2007

1 3 5 7 9 8 6 4 2
Copyright © Frank Ryan 2007

The rights of Frank Ryan to be identified as the Author of this Work have been asserted by him in accordance with the Copyright, Designs and Patents Act 1988

A catalogue record for this book is available from the British Library
ISBN 978-1-874082-43-9

All rights reserved. No part of this publication may be reproduced, stored in a retrieval system, or transmitted, in any form or by any means, electronic, mechanical, photocopying, recording or otherwise, without the prior permission of the publisher, nor be otherwise circulated in any form of binding or cover other than that in which it is published and without a similar condition including this condition being imposed on the subsequent purchaser.

Swift Publishers
PO Box 1436, Sheffield S17 3XP

e-mail: bookenquiries@swiftpublishers.com

Cover from a photo image of Brighton West Pier by Christopher Holt, reworked by Joanne Stubs and Andy Gallacher

Printed and bound by CPI Antony Rowe, Eastbourne

Hadya no more to do?
Was your work all done?
Had ya seen your first son?
Why'dya leave us all here?
Has the battle been won?

Allen Ginsberg:
        Elegy for Neal Cassidy

For Amy

1

When I was very small I had an obsession with the sea. It was a problem for my Mum and Dad who only had to let me out of their sight for a moment and I was off, stubby legs pumping over the sand and heading straight for that dangerous embrace. Here, tonight, I feel the reawakening of that compulsive need as I gaze down at the shifting surf about my legs, my feet already numb so that I am no longer aware of the coldness of the water, no longer aware that I am still wearing boots and socks or the wetness of my skin beneath my jeans. I am aware, without the slightest sense of strangeness, of the ghostly figures that have come to stand in the water beside me. There is more than one kind of ghost.

'What happened, Mylie?'

I say nothing.

The voice is that of my mother, Brenda, who is standing there next to my uncle, Tony.

Tony is wearing his Johnny Cash rug. Underneath the rug Tony has that shiny baldness you see in some men at an early age, especially those who lose at gambling. Normally when I see Tony I can't take my eyes off his bald head because I worry about my own hair. I have thick hair that is hard to control, but I still worry that one of these days I'll look at myself in the mirror and I'll see that same bald head shining back at me.

'Will you look at the state of him!' Tony says. 'I hope he knows the trouble he's in.'

It is only half a dream. I am floating between two worlds. My feet stand in the English Channel. Out there, beyond the horizon – invisible, although my eyes turn slowly towards it – is France. Above my dizzy, inebriated head is the starry sky of deepest night.

With another turn of my head, I gaze back towards the distant figure of Harry, cloaked in shadow, by the embers of last night's fire on the beach. I think about the Hindu concept of Kismet, which is another word for fate.

I say nothing.

About a month ago, there was a programme on Channel 4 that captured my imagination. It was a nature programme, one of those I like to watch. I had just arrived back at The Palace from working earlies and missed the start but I could see that it was going to be interesting. It was about a river in Australia whose banks had burst during heavy rain, and in the banks of the river lived some colonies of spiders. It was really incredible: there were millions upon millions of these spiders. They lived in burrows under the ground but when the river burst its banks it flooded the spiders' burrows. You'd have thought they were done for.

But the spiders swarmed up out of their holes in the ground. You should have seen them, scrambling up the tall reeds, where they began to spin their webs. These covered the banks, all running together until they became one huge cloud of silk floating over the landscape as far as the eye could see.

I watched this with a growing sense of wonder.

If you were a spider and you had to climb up those tall reeds to spin your webs, it must seem as if you had gone to live in the clouds. The spiders just floated on the breeze in what turned out to be their new home. They captured grasshoppers and other bugs to eat and they went on with their lives, safe from the floods that had washed away their burrows down in the ground.

2

They say that there is never truly a beginning to a story, only a convenient place to start. I suppose that for me this has to be the day when I first met Harry. As a matter of fact I remember it pretty well. It was a freezing day in February of this year, so bitter that frost had etched a diamantine lacery over the sixty yards of glazed corridor that links the Unit with the main hospital as I was walking back along it from the pharmacy, bringing some take-home drugs for the early discharges. The time was exactly a quarter past nine in the morning and Oasis', *Don't Look Back In Anger*, was running in my mind. Then, when I arrived at the Unit, I couldn't get through the glass doors because Harry was blocking the entrance into the reception area.

Of course I didn't know at the time that his name was Harry. I knew nothing about him, except that he was a new admission. And to be accurate, he wasn't just lying there. There were six people sitting on him.

I want to get it right.

He was fighting like a madman, shouting and cursing at the top of his voice, and they were holding on to various bits of him. Alan was in charge of it, holding on to his head, and John and Rachel were holding on to his arms, with Barry, Jill and Janet holding on to his legs. I had to inch my way through one door sideways and then pick my step around them in order to drop the drugs off at the desk before I could make my way to the kitchen.

I'm no good to anybody until I get my first mug of tea in the morning. And one of Mary's attempts at escaping had caused me to miss out on it when I had arrived, deliberately early, at a quarter to seven.

Ann, who works regular earlies, unlocked the kitchen door for me and ushered me in. She didn't give a damn about my tea. Instead she followed me around the room, talking in this nagging voice, while I was putting on the kettle for the hot water, and putting the teabag into the mug. Ann is a middle-aged Scottish woman, who wears the permanent mask of a frown. The thing was, I was still enjoying the music. It's something I like to do, just hang loose with it inside my head while I'm going through some menial routine. But Ann wouldn't let me do that. She was telling me how tired Doctor Henessy must be, after being up half the night as the SHO on call.

It was Doctor Henessy who was talking to the old man on the floor and Ann told me she was getting nowhere.

I like Doctor Henessy, whose first name is Margaret. To be honest with you, she's my favourite amongst the doctors. Everybody, with the exception of old Grumpy, calls her Maggie.

Although Ann is only an enrolled nurse, I respect her opinion when it comes to patients. She had worked it out that the reason Maggie was getting nowhere was because the old man had been brought in after trying to strangle his wife. It was what you might call a gender situation. So there she was, laying this conscience thing on me. She said,

'You know you have a way with the old men, Mylie.'

'Hey!' I grinned. 'Winning – or wicked?'

'Mischievous!' said she, pronouncing it 'mis-chee-vious'. But her mask had wrinkled into the hint of a smile.

Outside Reception, patients were hanging about the upholstered chairs that visitors normally sit in. They're always interested in what's going on.

It was obvious the old man couldn't just stay there on the floor. Normally, the ward staff are very kind to patients. All they were doing was stopping him from escaping while at the same time making sure he didn't hurt himself. I found myself having to squat down on the floor close to his head so I could talk to him.

'C–D–O,' Alan was mouthing to me above the commotion, which means the old man was coming in as a compulsory detention order under the Mental Health Act.

The way it usually happens is that a qualified psychiatric nurse, known as a Court Diversion Officer, does a round of the police cells each morning and picks out the obvious mental cases. The old man couldn't have been too hard to spot after they had pulled him in the night before for trying to strangle his wife. In fact John, who is the Court Diversion Officer, was one of the six people holding him down. I could see that the old man hadn't shaved for a couple of days. He had a thick white moustache and a bald head - a floury kind of baldness unlike the shiny baldness of my Uncle Tony - and he was wearing a crumpled pinstripe suit that looked as if he had slept in it. Nobody likes to be brought into a psychiatric unit against their will. It's an infringement of their civil liberties. The old man's face was blotchy and the only one of his eyes I could see was his right eye, because the other half of his face was pressed against the floor. You have never seen such a fierce-looking eye! It was a perfect blue, like the blazing spearhead of a Bunsen burner flame. And it was staring back at me.

'Hello,' I said, although it must have been hard for him to hear me above the noise of his own cursing and swearing. 'You don't look very comfortable down there. Why don't you stop fighting us and let us help you.'

'Bugger off!' he muttered back at me.

I've seen this rage before and so I took no notice of it. His voice was slurred because half his mouth was pressed up tightly against the carpet.

Then I saw the bowler hat. It really took me by surprise. It was lying on its side about six feet away across the floor and I realised that it must have fallen off his head. I crawled over, on my hands and knees, to pick it up. I had never held a real bowler hat in my hands before and I was curious, that's all. Anyway, I could see that this hat meant a lot to the old man, so I brushed it off with my sleeve and put it down on the floor next to the mug of tea - my mug of tea. I took some trouble arranging the mug and hat so they were easy for him to see. All the time he was watching me through that bright blue eye of his. I had to pick up my voice a little, to make sure I was getting through to him. 'Do you see that tea there next to your hat?'

'Piss off!'

It isn't easy trying to communicate with somebody in that situation. His voice was becoming even more squashed as he tried to shout and curse through the dust-speckled bubbles of spit that were dangling from the free corner of his mouth.

'I haven't had a sip out of that tea,' I moved myself closer to his ear. 'I made it for myself.' I faced him down, that mad look in his eye. 'You're welcome to it if you will just give over all that shouting and swearing.'

I pride myself on being a philosophical kind of person, but you should have seen the glare in his eye!

His white hair, what little there was of it, was dishevelled and covered in dust. But I just knew in my bones how much he was dying for that mug of tea.

'We're not getting very far, are we?' I said to him. We were all waiting while Maggie was considering if she needed to give the old man an injection. We prefer to avoid it if we can. And you have to give them a test dose first to make sure the sedative doesn't cause an adverse reaction. I felt an urgent need to stretch my back at this point because I was half-kneeling in the most awkward position you can imagine, bending down to get close to him.

'You swine!' he gargled through his spit.

It was such a comical thing for him to say that I couldn't help laughing. I know I shouldn't have laughed and maybe that was why his eye screwed up and a tear came out of it.

'Hey – come on, now! You're among friends here.' I took the clean tissue from Ann and wiped his eye for him. Then I wiped him down over the visible half of his face.

'I think you can let his head go now,' I said to Alan. 'It looks as if he's calming down.'

You can imagine how undignified it must feel having your face shoved against the floor. Alan let go of his head and the old man screwed it around on his neck so he could take a good long look at me with two mad eyes instead of one. I could hear his neck cracking like an old clockwork mechanism as it turned. That gave me the chance to wipe the dirt off the other side of his face. I was glad we didn't need to inject him.

So there I was, helping him change his clothes while he was drinking my tea and looking very forlorn on the two mattresses on the floor, when suddenly he said to me, 'Young man, my wife is a bitch.'

It sounded strange to hear him speak so crudely of his wife in his clipped middle-class accent. Of course this started me off laughing again. I just couldn't help myself because it sounded so incongruous. 'That bloody woman!' He went on. 'When I get out of here I'm going to murder her!'

'That's cool,' I murmured, humouring him while I gathered up the pinstripe for cleaning. Harry was a short man, maybe five eight, but he was in pretty good shape – surprisingly well toned for his age. I could see that he would cut a smart figure still in his pinstripe and bowler hat. You wouldn't think he was suffering from any physical or mental illness. He was wearing a sweat-stained shirt, with silver cufflinks, under his jacket. Somebody had cut a hole out of the right armpit of his shirt. I paused to ask him about that as I unbuttoned the shirt, making a knot of the two cufflinks and sliding them into the left side jacket pocket. He informed me, in a furtive kind of a voice, that he suffered from terrible pains in his arm after an attack of shingles. 'I can't bear anything to touch me there,' he said, 'not even to brush against the hairs in my armpit.'

'You should try to calm down a little,' I murmured, trying to be friendly. I have a deep voice that seems to soothe some people. 'Why don't you just rest now for a while? Maybe get some sleep. Then, when you wake up, things might look different. You never know, things might even start to make sense again.'

Some people manage to do that straight away after they have been admitted. It just seems to click them into focus and they get things sorted out inside their head.

The fact was, Harry – his name is Harold Edward Severn by the way but we like to call people by their first names – didn't even watch as I added his bowler hat to the pile of clothes that needed to go to the laundry. I have been borrowing a book or two from Alan and Michael and I have been learning about the subconscious mind. I see it as an inner landscape in which we each have this deep well, a sort of well of life, and this is the reason why we'll fight like hell to survive. Harry had sunk right down to the bottom of his well. And that was why he didn't give a damn anymore.

I took off his shoes (because of the laces) and his tie and braces for the same reason. The pills - and he had several varieties of them - I put to one side to pass on to Alan when I got back to the nurses' station.

Dressed in ward pyjamas, poor old Harry was looking a little bit shocked. I had another rummage in the bag he must have packed for himself when the police arrived to take him away. I didn't learn much about him from the contents of that bag. Apart from his medication, I discovered nothing except his razor and a toothbrush. I left him the toothbrush and added the razor to the pile I was taking.

I am forgetting – there was one other thing, a single old book with yellowed pages. It was about the size of a Gideon's Bible. I squinted at the cover as I put it down on the mattress beside him. It was the only other thing I could let him keep from the contents of his bag. It was by a writer called Arthur Koestler. The title was *Darkness at Noon*.

Maybe Harry would have felt better if I could have left him on his own for a while. He could have put his head down and reflected on things. Unfortunately, I couldn't just let him do this.

Doctor Henessy – Maggie – had put him on 'CNOs', which means constant nursing observations. CNOs can't be left on their own even to go to the toilet. And I wasn't just being inquisitive then, looking through Harry's personal things. He had been admitted to what is called a 'Safe Room' on the first floor ward we call 'Gerries'. This room has no glass: the window is a double plastic laminate, which is unbreakable, like the panel in the door. There are no plug sockets he could stick a piece of metal into and electrocute himself. The light is also unbreakable and flush with the ceiling. Harry was a 'DSH', which means at risk of deliberate self harm. I carried his things out into the corridor and handed them to Michael and then I fetched a chair back out of the dining room and wedged it in the open door, so I could keep an eye on him.

There's an interesting idea the psychiatrists call a key stimulus, by which they mean an emotional trigger. You could regard it as the detonator on a mental time bomb. For Harry I assumed this would have something to do with his wife. Put him near her, put even the thought of her into his mind, and he wanted to murder her. But now, separated from her and with this calming situation around him, there was a chance that the normal Harry might show through.

3

Let me tell you – and I'm doing my best to keep my language under control – I'm having some trouble with the system right now. And that's why I had to beg ten minutes cover from Michael so I could go and see Brian.

The way we work it, there are two shifts, earlies and lates. Earlies begin at seven in the morning and finish at three o'clock. Lates begin at two and finish at ten o'clock in the evening. There's a half hour break for lunch. On earlies, this is at twelve noon, if you're lucky. On lates, it's at six-thirty in the evening. Of course other people work things differently.

There are day staff, like Anna on Reception, and there are the Night Owls, who work regular nights. I don't know if they get extra pay for that, but if they do, they deserve it.

The problem, for me at least, is getting my fair share of weekends off.

I'm not a whinger. A lot of the work on a psychiatric ward is tedious. It's a funny thing, but I don't mind even the most boring routines. I can't say I like shovelling shit, but there isn't much of that, not like on a long-stay geriatric ward. On the whole I like working on the Unit more than I would have thought when I began here five months ago.

For example, if Harry had wanted to talk to me, I'd have been happy to listen. I've always been a good listener. My Uncle Tony says that it's because I have a curiosity for people like a vacuum cleaner has for dirt. But I prefer to see it as an empathic quality. It's in my nature to empathise with people.

But I can't be doing with losing my free weekends.

Weekends off are like gold dust. We take it in turns to work weekends and only one of the three Health Care Assistants gets Saturday and Sunday off at a time. Most months I just get a single weekend off but this month, unusually - fantastically - it is two. Enter old Billy Welsh and his very convenient bad back. With just the two of us left working, I lose one of my two weekends – or so Admin would like to think.

That was why I cadged ten minutes off from specialing Harry so I could go to see Brian on the ground floor.

Brian is about thirty years old. He was wearing the usual dark grey suit, a white shirt and a shades-of-red silk tie.

'I thought you would be pleased to get the overtime,' he said to me.

'Not if it means I don't get my two weekends this month.' I made no secret of the fact that I was well and truly brassed off with him. 'I've made plans for every single free weekend for the next two or three months.'

In fact I never make plans for anything, but that's none of his business. It was just another part of my strategy of battering down hard on his head. Letting him see that he wasn't going to get away with this.

'When you contracted to be employed by us, you agreed to work with the vicissitudes of the system.'

'Vicissitudes my eye!' I said to him. 'Look, Brian! If you can get by without me, then you can just give me my cards.'

'There's no need for this kind of confrontation.'

'Do you think there will be a queue of people outside your door, willing to work these shifts for the wages you pay me?'

'It's no problem,' said he, somewhat red-faced. 'We'll go to the banking agency.'

No problem! Why the hell didn't he think of the banking agency before he tried to rob me of my second weekend!

Grumpy came to see Harry at twelve o'clock. Grumpy is the name we give to Doctor Alasdair Dury, who is the senior psychiatrist on the Unit.

He's about sixty years old. You can be sure that he didn't thank me for the way I had helped the nursing staff handle his patient. He doesn't call us health care assistants, or HCAs. He calls us orderlies. Whatever you call us, HCAs or orderlies, we are at the bottom of the heap in the National Health Service. We are the bums of the system. You require no training at all to become a health care assistant, so people like Grumpy can crap on you whenever they feel like it.

Maybe I was still feeling angry from my encounter with Brian half an hour earlier, and it didn't help that Grumpy's lateness was delaying my lunch break. But I have to admit that Grumpy was very patient with Harry.

There are three psychiatrists working on the Psychiatric Unit, and Grumpy is the most old-fashioned. He is what they call a post-Freudian psychoanalyst, as well as being a psycho-geriatrician. Grumpy thinks the main thing is to let people talk to him for as long as they want. Sometimes I think he goes to sleep while they are talking because his eyelids droop and he says nothing. What that means is his interviews can drag on for hours. He grunts a lot, which makes you think he's snoring, and he even belches now and then while he's with his patients. Once I actually saw him lift one cheek off the chair and sneakily fart.

I had hoped to get off the CNOs for my lunch while Grumpy was there but he told me to move inside and close the door. Listening in to the interview I did learn some interesting details about Harry. I discovered that he was a retired businessman, a work-study engineer. It was his dog that had made him want to strangle his wife. The dog was the detonator on Harry's mental bomb.

Harry didn't even deny what he had done. In fact he talked about it as if it were the most natural thing in the world.

'Muriel wouldn't let me do it,' he said in a flat tone of voice. 'She kept slapping my face.'

Muriel, it seems, is the name of Harry's wife. I wouldn't be at all surprised after that if Muriel has a notion in her head to get rid of Harry.

Anyway, from what he was saying, he tried to strangle her off and on over several hours before she got fed up with him and called the police.

The thing that really did upset him – the emotional trigger – was the fact that Muriel had had his dog put down when he went away to Brighton for a few days' holiday. He wept when he told Grumpy that, because he wished he had taken the dog with him.

'Before she got arthritic,' he said, 'I used to take Nobby with me for company. We'd go down to Brighton in my car. We liked to walk along the beach together.'

The dog was a little Scottish terrier. It sounded to me as if Nobby had got so decrepit that Muriel must have been waiting for the chance to get rid of her. I mean, it sounded as if Muriel was jealous of Harry's dog.

4

The Unit is part of the District General Hospital in the sense that it shares the same grounds and there is a corridor that links them, but when you go in through those twin glass doors you might as well be landing on the moon.

One reason for this is that people can stay here for up to six months. People come in here to live for a while. This is where they come to escape those flooded burrows down on the ground.

Nobody in the building wears any kind of a uniform, not even the consultants. They dress in ordinary clothes. As far as the nurses are concerned, I'm talking about jeans and sweatshirts or pullovers, so it can be difficult at first to tell the nurses from the patients. The doctors tend to look a bit more formal. For example my favourite, Maggie, always looks smart in a dark skirt or trousers. The consultants are the only ones who wear suits. That's if you regard the double-breasted shaggy jackets with the odd button missing and the crumpled trousers that Grumpy wears as suits. There is a garden where some of the patients work and a gym and a Day Centre, with its own badminton court. So you get the picture. It has to be different, otherwise the patients would feel lost when they went back into the world outside.

There are three wards, one downstairs where you also find the offices, and two upstairs, one of which is for Gerries – which is psychogeriatrics.

The ward on the bottom is Joseph Mallord William Turner, where, according to reputation, the patients are said to be all 'bad'. Upstairs you find John Constable, where they are all 'mad'. And finally, of course, there is William Blake, also known as Gerries, where they are both 'mad and bad'.

You enter through a vestibule with big glass windows and on your right is a map of the Unit and a machine selling soft drinks and chocolates. You just walk on through the second pair of doors, inside which you find Reception. This is where Harry was fighting everybody when he came in.

Reception is carpeted in blues and greys. Everybody smiles at Anna, who is sitting there behind her desk. She works the dayshift hours, which are nine to five. Anna is not to be confused with Ann. No way could anybody possibly confuse them, once they had met Anna. Anna is the sexiest woman in the world. She's Dutch, about five eight and has platinum blonde hair to about an inch below her chin.

Even old Grumpy must be lusting after Anna.

Anna is carrying out a staff integration exercise of her own. But we all have to take our place in the queue because she's working her way through the male nurses, giving them what she calls her 'counselling'. I dream about being counselled by Anna so today, as usual, I gave her a bit of a smile when I arrived and passed by her desk.

'Hi, Anna!'

Anna reached out and ruffled my hair.

'Hiya, Antonio Banderas!' she called out, laughing. You wouldn't believe how she gets on my nerves with that kind of thing at times.

Past Reception you find the offices for secretaries, Admin. and the consultants, which are separate from their outpatient consulting rooms. I forgot to mention there's a Computer Office, where some of the records are kept. Then, at the bottom of the corridor just before you get to Turner, there's the Treatment Suite. This is where I spent most of this morning. But first I had to get away from Grumpy, who was on the warpath.

Grumpy is a bit touchy these days because of Dr Boyson's new book. Dr Boyson is Grumpy's main rival on the Unit. He has written a best-selling book called *Choices*, in which he argues the case for his liberal philosophy of life. Grumpy thinks liberal thinking like this has given rise to a society that would consider such a thing as euthanasia.

So old Grumpy and 'Choices' Boyson are feudin' doctors, if only in a very English kind of a way. They make a point of not speaking to each other when they meet on the wards.

Anyway, what had set the fuse today was the fact that some doctor had told the papers that he helped at least fifty of his patients to die.

Grumpy was waving his morning paper about in the nurses' office.

'They want doctors to become bloody executioners!' he said.

I hadn't taken much notice of the euthanasia debate before, to be honest with you, but old Grumpy got me interested.

So I read the article after Grumpy had stormed off to his clinic. I also had a good look at the picture of this slate-wiper of patients. To me he just looked like a white-haired old man, climbing out of his car for a routine day at the office. It seems that this doctor had helped a woman suffering from motor neurone disease to die. Motor neurone disease is a really horrible condition where you get more and more paralysed while your brain remains active. This poor woman had reached the point where she could no longer speak or swallow. So the doctor gave her twenty times the normal dose of a sleeping tablet called Temazepam and supplied her with a large plastic bag, known as a 'customized exit bag', which is the size of a dustbin liner and has an adhesive neck seal.

'The patient took an overdose of Temazepam and the plastic bag was then involved,' he explained to the reporter. 'That is a way you can guarantee death.'

No kidding!

I got so interested in reading the paper that I was a little late leaving the nurses office and I had to hurry to help out on the Treatment Suite.

I like working on the Treatment Suite, which is the psychiatric equivalent of an operating theatre. This is where we give some of the really sick patients electric shock therapy. I know that there are people who don't agree with this kind of treatment. They think it's barbaric, making sick people have fits in order to treat them. Before I came to work here I probably felt the same because I had never seen people who were really sick in their minds. I had some vague idea they were just a bit nervous or depressed, a little worse than I feel myself with a hangover. It was a shock for me to come face to face with what it is really like to blow your mind.

The junior doctors, who are called Senior House Officers or 'SHOs', give the shock therapy for their consultants, who always seem to be too busy. But there has to be an anaesthetist knocking them out first. This morning the anaesthetist was Doctor Ruth Thompson, who is aged about fifty with dyed red hair, and the SHO was my favourite, Maggie, looking cute in a creamy blouse and black skirt. It often seems to be Maggie who is asked to give the patients their therapeutic shocks. She once told me that she has been through feminism and come out the other side, whatever that means.

'How are you?' she said to me with her busy little smile. Maggie is always friendly to me. She has dark curly hair, cut short, like a boy's.

'Struggling!' I returned the smile.

If it wasn't for Tabi I could fall truly, madly and deeply in love with Maggie. It isn't just the fact that she's an intelligent woman, it's the fierceness about the way she cares for her patients.

There can be as many as three patients on these sessions, which take place on Tuesday or, as today, on a Friday morning. I had to go up to William Blake to fetch an old lady who was waiting there in a wheelchair. She was a really frail person, tiny and thin, with that waxy kind of sweat you notice about them, and there was a dressing around her throat where the surgeons had sewn her up after she tried to kill herself. Her name was Mrs Feinstein – Freda.

I gave her a smile and said, 'Good morning, Freda.' I try not to be too boisterous with people because I want to be respectful, even though I like to pull their legs.

Freda didn't respond at all. Her eyes were staring. Nothing was moving, not even her eyelids. They had put cellulose drops in her eyes to stop her corneas ulcerating. Maggie, who met up with us at the lift and walked with us along the corridor to the Treatment Suite, told me that if ECT couldn't do the trick she didn't know what would.

She explained to me, in a whisper that caused her breath to brush against my ear, 'Her mind is paralysed, just like her muscles.'

That idea really startled me.

So, along the way, Maggie told me more about Freda's condition, a complication called depressive retardation, when all your muscles turn to lead.

Freda had cut her throat because of a thirty-pound gas bill, when she had thousands in the bank.

'We've tried everything else and nothing has helped her. All the tablets and injections, even feeding her through a central line that goes through a vein in her neck and straight into the right atrium of her heart.'

Maggie didn't need to justify the electric shock treatment to me. I could see that Freda was going to die unless the shock treatment cured her.

It's not entirely accidental that I came to work in the Psychiatric Unit. I'm interested in all aspects of mental illness, including electric shock treatment. That's why I volunteer to help out in the Treatment Suite whenever they want me.

There's a waiting room with walls and ceiling the blue of a summer sky over a carpet the colour of a hayfield. The fitter patients walk into the room and then wait for the anaesthetist in an upholstered chair with wooden arms. Freda sat patiently in her wheelchair. I stayed behind, helping out Maggie and the anaesthetist, Doctor Thompson, until Freda was coming round again after the electric shock had blasted away the depressive cobwebs from her brain.

Then, afterwards, I watched while Maggie wrote the details into the notes and filled in the chart.

After ECT one of the experienced nurses comes into the recovery room and does a cognitive function assessment, to make sure there is no brain damage. Today it was Karim Patel who arrived to do the assessment. It always amazes me how the patient wakes up within a minute or so of the fit and how soon they are able to start the assessment after that.

Karim helped me to turn Freda over on to her side on the trolley and then I took her through into the recovery room.

When I lifted Freda back into the wheelchair, she wasn't like a statue any more. She was slumped over to her left side with her head down on a floppy neck and Karim, who speaks with a quiet Pakistani accent, started going through the list of questions. All Freda spoke was three words. She whispered in this croaky little voice, 'Thank you, Doctor,' no matter what question the nurse tried to ask her.

So there I was, rolling her back in her chair to the ward, and she said the same thing to me. I was just explaining to her, 'Freda – I am going to take you over the bump into the lift.'

Then she said it to me, without ever lifting her head up from that dropped-down position: 'Thank you, Doctor.'

It really made me feel good. I know it's only a small thing but it made me feel that even the bum of the system could make some kind of a contribution.

5

I parked the wheelchair in the cubicle next to the linen cupboard and then I checked with Michael to see if it was all right for me to go and see Harry.

Michael is the Ward Manager on William Blake. He's positively ancient amongst the male nurses, at fifty years old. He is also gay, with a dozen gold studs in his ears, and his hair hangs down in a wide tail on the back of his neck in the style known as a mullet.

He said it was okay for me to go in and have a few words with Harry. In fact he seemed to appreciate the gesture.

It seems sad to me that not a single friend or relative – Muriel included – has come to see Harry since his admission to the Unit.

Harry has been moved out of the Safe Room and into a side ward, to allow him time on his own to acclimatise to the ward routine. I knocked very lightly on the door before I entered, but he didn't appear to notice me at all. He was dozing in his chair beside the window. That's the trouble when you put somebody on antidepressant drugs. The drugs can make people sleepy. Sometimes they can make patients so confused they are rambling out of their skulls.

Harry had slumped down to the right and I had to prop him up in the chair so that he wouldn't injure himself. While I was doing so I saw that the book had fallen out of his hand. It was lying on the carpet with the pages turned down, still open at the place he had stopped reading.

I picked up the book and I went to put it on top of his locker. But I didn't want him to lose track of his progress and so I glanced at it while I was considering how to mark the page. There was a name written down in faded ink on the blank pages just inside the cover: *R. Giles*. It surprised me that it wasn't Harry's name. I began to feel guilty because it all seemed very personal to him. At the same time I couldn't help thinking about this person called Giles, who had written his name inside the cover of Harry's book. It would never have occurred to me to do something like that. So I was starting to wonder if a book would have to have some really special kind of meaning for somebody to write his name in it. I almost put it down right then but instead I still held it in my hands. The yellowed pages looked as if they had been read and re-read. I didn't know if it was Harry or this person called Giles who had found the book so interesting. I had never had the opportunity to read *Darkness at Noon*. But now I saw that Harry had reached page 109, a chapter called, THE SECOND HEARING. My eye caught a snatch of conversation:

> *'Now do you believe me?' whispered No 406, and smiled at him happily. Rubashov nodded. Then the old man's face darkened: Rubashov recognized the expression of fear, which fell on him every time he was shut into his cell.*

The words startled me. I wondered if this was how Harry looked upon his admission to the Unit. I wondered if he also felt as if he was shut away inside his cell.

There was a blue meals menu on top of the locker so I folded this in half and put it into the book to mark the page for him. Then I closed the book, still holding it in my hands. I looked down at the worn cover, which had a picture of the man I presumed was Rubashov, though you couldn't be at all sure what he looked like because the face on the cover had been deliberately scratched out. It was a dark cover, with tones that were all shades of midnight. I couldn't help but wonder about the connection between Giles and Harry. I had been so convinced that nobody but Harry had ever read that book. All that wear, all those thumbed pages. I put it down carefully on the top of his locker.

Suddenly Harry started shouting at the top of his voice, with his eyes staring.

There weren't any real words to the shout. It was more of a howling, to be honest with you.

He looked like he was taking hold of something really tight in his right fist. He was climbing up out of his chair. There was such a wild look in his eyes. I thought he was throwing something out of his right hand, or at least he was throwing it in his imagination, out of the clenched fist of his right hand.

He was making such a racket that I tried to calm him down and then Michael popped his head around the door to check what was going on.

'It's all right,' I said, chuckling. 'He's only dreaming. Some kind of nightmare.'

Michael told me to wake him up. I made the mistake of shaking his right shoulder, forgetting that this was the side where he had had the shingles. So he started cursing and swearing and muttering, 'Oh, the pain – the pain!'

'Hey – I'm sorry, Harry,' I said, straightening him out in the chair. 'Would you like me to get you something? A cup of tea or a newspaper?'

'Who the hell are you?'

'Don't you remember me?'

Harry has a habit I have noticed with quite a few of the patients. He refuses to look you in the eyes. Even now, in response to my question, he only gave me a sideways glance, when those bright blue eyes barely flickered in my direction.

'The tea wallah!' he barked.

'Yeah, that's me,' I laughed, shifting uneasily on the edge of his bed. 'So you do remember? My name is Mylie.'

'What kind of a name is that?'

'Mylie O'Farrell,' I added.

'Sounds like an Irish name to me.'

'I come from Sheffield.'

'Sheffield?'

'Yeah, you've heard of Sheffield,' I muttered, because he had said it with that tone of voice I have sometimes encountered with Londoners. 'It's either the fourth or the fifth biggest city in England, depending where you place Manchester. I'm not sure that even Manchester knows exactly where to place Manchester.'

'No need to get touchy!' he said. 'I know where Sheffield is.'

'Yeah!'

'I know all about Sheffield,' he said, making a point of not looking me in the eyes again. 'The Independent Socialist Republic of South Yorkshire.'

I didn't bother to correct him, although times have changed. Sheffield is more of a Liberal Democrat city these days. 'There was a time,' I said, 'when more than half of the quality steel in the world was made in Sheffield.'

'Is that so?' he answered, looking into the distance.

'Yeah, as a matter of fact it is!'

It's the kind of thing that gives you a pretty good feeling, if you were born in Sheffield. What made me mad was the fact that it didn't matter a damn to Harry.

6

South of the Marylebone flyover you find the rich Arabs, who are willing to pay upwards of a thousand pounds a week for a single apartment so they can stay the summer in London and escape the heat back home. North of the flyover is where I live, in a puce-brick terraced house off the Edgware Road, sandwiched between the blocks of Westminster Council flats, and with an entrance off a grimy tunnel. This is the residence I share with my friends, Janus and Rich. Here we pay two hundred pounds a week for the entire house. We call it 'The Palace'.

I was still feeling pretty wound up as I was headed back there on the 98 bus. Along the way, I called in at the Church Street market, where I bought a crinkly lettuce, tomatoes and a cucumber from an Edwardian stall on iron-shod wheels. When I got in, I made myself a bowl of pasta to go with the salad and sat down alone at the scarred wooden table in the living room. Then I made a mug of tea, carried it upstairs to my room and I played Corinne Bailey Ray on my I-pod. Some music sounds better loud from a player, so it fills the room. But the mood I was in was I-pod personal.

Corinne is really going places fast. This is her first CD, which has just her name and her image, looking kind of cute and awkward, in a shoe-string-strap black dress, on the cover. I wouldn't even know how to start to describe her voice, other than to say it is vulnerable-in-trouble-rusty-magical, like Billy Holiday reborn.

Although it was just afternoon, it felt like wounded midnight to me, and she assuaged my wound. What I was thinking about was Tabi's father, Doctor Mather, who used to say that Sheffield was an ugly picture in a beautiful frame. I know what he meant by it: the beautiful frame is the Derbyshire Dales. But I wouldn't have talked about Sheffield like that. The trouble with people is they have to make boxes so they can put their ideas into them.

To tell you the truth, I was still cursing Harry's existence. It wasn't just the tone of his voice when he had said 'Sheffield' like that. It was the way he had told me I had an Irish name, like it was some kind of a disadvantage or something.

I was born from the union of a Sheffield mother and an Irish father. I don't remember too much about my father, Tommy, because he died from a cerebral haemorrhage when I was eight years old. I remember a lot more about my Irish grandfather, Patrick, because I once stayed with him in Ireland during the long summer holidays. Patrick was the first of the O'Farrell family to come to England. He came over from Ireland during the war and he volunteered to join the army. I don't know why he did that, when he didn't need to. All I know is that he came from a place called Tramore, which is a seaside resort on the southern Irish coastline. After the war he went back to Tramore but later his two sons, Tommy and Tony, followed his example and came to England, and they ended up in Sheffield looking for work. Tommy became a steelworker and married my mother, Brenda, while Tony went into my grandfather's taxi business, back then, when my English grandfather was still alive. So there you have it, the O'Farrell family history, and you can work it out for yourself that I am half Irish and half Sheffield steel.

But this is all getting slightly boring and so I am not going to say any more about it except that I can imagine what my father saw in my mother.

Mum and I have things in common. She is inclined to be very stubborn. That's one way in which I take after my mother. I also take after her in my looks. Mum is dark enough to be Italian. That's the reason I tan easily and why I have a thick head of blue-black hair.

People think it's a big deal having black wavy hair. I know they talk about the ideal man as being tall (I am six-one) and dark and handsome. I have the dark bit all right, but I don't think I'm quite there on the handsome. And being dark has its disadvantages. For example, if I really want to look clean-faced I have to shave twice a day.

I used to think I was what they call an angry young man until I met Janus.

I don't know why I got on to talking about Janus. I really don't want to talk about that madman right now, to be honest with you. Instead I would like to explain some of the great influences in my life. These are the people I call my stepping stones. The people I am talking about are Bob Marley, Bertrand Russell and Leonardo da Vinci. Now I know this might seem a peculiar kind of a list to you, but there are good reasons why I picked them.

For example, I like da Vinci because in spite of the fact that he was such an arrogant man he had a really inventive mind. It's funny, when you think about it, how many of these geniuses were also a little bit crazy. I am thinking also of Bertrand Russell, leching after his housemaids, and Isaac Newton, who worked out the exact date of the Day of Judgement.

Of course, most of the time I don't bother to shave twice a day. The only time I ever did was when I was going out with Tabi. She was my girlfriend back in

Sheffield. She's about five nine tall, with straight brown hair. I don't know how it is now but she used to have long hair about halfway down her back.

Most people would think she is beautiful. I know I certainly do. I get wound up when I am thinking about Tabi, so I have to be careful what I say.

I'm not going to say anything more about her right now except to explain that there were people who didn't like the fact that Tabi and I were seeing each other. To a certain extent I can't blame them. Tabi comes from the Ecclesall Road and I come from the Abbeydale Road. The lawyers and doctors live in Ecclesall and the taxi drivers live down in Abbeydale. But there was another and even better reason why they didn't like our going out together: I had a bit of a reputation when it came to girls.

Tabi went to the same comprehensive school as me. She was always in the top two or three of the class and I was usually somewhere near the bottom. I'm not blaming the teachers, who were mostly all right, but they have to teach what they are told to teach and I suspect they are as bored with it as I was. I must have been a great disappointment to my mother, who hoped I was another Einstein. That's mums for you, I suppose.

Once in my life I wrote an essay that got ten out of ten in English. It was when I had a probationary teacher you could have a bit of a laugh with. I got along with him really well. He told me I could just go ahead and write about whatever interested me for a change and so I talked about Sheffield and the stupid way my father had died and about how my Uncle Tony sold his house and brought his family to live next door to us. He did that when he was really short of money. I thought it was a nice thing to do when my mum was going around the bend with grief.

The truth is I was always in some kind of bother at school. I didn't do criminal things – nothing like that. It was just the fact I wasn't interested.

I suppose it's also true that I came down to London because of Tabi, although I haven't ever tried to get in touch.

Tabi is a first year student at the Queen Mary and Westfield College, which is one of about a thousand colleges all over London that are connected with London University. Before I met her, I had had quite a few girlfriends, or half a dozen anyway, that my friends used to say were dogs. I think that's a tragic way to talk about anybody. One of these girls was Alison Morley. She was two years older than me, a sixth-form Art student, who made casts of her body for her A-level project. I walked her home one night after a disco. We had both knocked back our fair share of lager and the walk to her place was too long for my bladder to wait. In my embarrassment, I had to turn down a small alleyway to get relief. I knew nothing about girls then. I didn't know if she would be disgusted, or even if she would wait for me. You can imagine how surprised I was when I returned to find her pirouetting, a little bit unsteadily, under the street light, her hands stretched out to either side and her eyes and mouth wide open to the rain. She was laughing like a maniac.

She was a bit of a wild case, was Alison, and she soon had me laughing with her. We did it behind her house, up against the backstreet wall in the rain. I had never had sex with anybody in my life before but she showed me what to do.

What I am saying is that neither of us made a big deal out of it. It seemed like a perfectly natural thing to do, like the logical conclusion to the two of us walking home together. And don't get any big ideas that I skanked her, pretending that I loved her or anything.

Nothing like that at all. Alison was a really nice person, no matter that some of my friends made barking sounds whenever she walked past at school after that. I was in my final year for GCSEs at the time, so I'd have been about sixteen years old. Okay – so she wouldn't have won any Miss World contest but she had a truly creative way of looking at life.

Those clever friends of mine, what they failed to grasp is that you can enjoy sex with an intelligent women, even if she isn't a film star. To tell you the truth, I remember Alison with a good deal more affection than I do those 'woof-woofing' friends.

Tabi of course was different.

I must have known Tabi just about as long as I can remember. She went to the same junior school as I did although we were never in the same group of friends. There was no kind of needle there, nothing like that. We just had different circles we moved in because Tabi's father was a doctor.

Everybody calls him mad Doctor Mather.

He had lost his wife years before, just as my mum had lost my dad, and he didn't bother to look after himself. My Uncle Tony said he was a sarcastic Scotch pig because he told him that his bones weren't filled with red marrow but with black ingratitude.

Tony can be a bit of a nuisance at times, when he's worrying about his heart. He's always thinking he's about to have a heart attack, when he has lost a bundle on the horses. Of course he doesn't ever come out and say that he's worrying about his heart. Instead he lies down on the couch saying he feels dizzy, or he has this pain that is killing him around his left nipple.

Doctor Mather has been my family's doctor ever since I was a baby. He runs what is called a one-man practice.

Everybody wants him to be their doctor, in spite of the fact that he's sarcastic. You should hear the way he curses you if you call him out at night! Tony was always calling him out with his complaints. I remember a time when Tony got into a panic about three in the morning and my mother sent me with him to Doctor Mather's house. Tony made me throw pebbles at the window. He was groaning and rolling around the place and whining that he was having a heart attack. I can still see the doctor's head poking out of the window on the first floor and I can hear him cursing down at my Uncle Tony:

'You've just about given me a heart attack, you hypochondriacal Irish shite!'

Doctor Mather is only crazy in the way people sometimes lose the plot of it as they get older, and he thinks the world of Tabi. He'd let her do just about anything she wanted to do, because he trusts her. I think it's cool when a father trusts his daughter like that.

I have often wondered why Tabi and I hit it off in the way we did - whether these things are Karma, as some people believe, or whether Karma is just another word for the chaos theory, which is a great favourite with my friend Janus.

Tabi has one of those beautiful faces, with a high forehead. She looks like a model with tits, to be really honest with you. I'm ashamed to admit that that was the image I had of her at that time.

With my being tall and shaving from an early age, I was spending most evenings with my friends in pubs and discos while Tabi, who is actually two months older than me, was working for her A-levels. Now and then, on the occasions we'd meet, it was clear, from the friendly banter we had between us, that she found me easy to talk to. She must have fancied me more than I thought from what she told me later, but of course I didn't know that then. Naturally I thought that her opinion of me was the same as everybody else's.

The reason we first got together in a deeper than friendly way, was accidental. It was during the Easter break, after we had taken the A-level mock exams, and we happened to meet at the rave where most of our year were getting bladdered. I must have thought she looked like she needed somebody to see her home. It was no bother since we only lived at opposite ends of the same road. We had to walk about three miles out of the city centre but it was a nice cool night in early April, if a little breezy. There was a pleasant kind of a feeling between us, although we didn't hold hands or link arms or anything. I can remember how the air felt like frost congealing on my skin and the sycamores were like columns of marching soldiers, swaying in the wind because they were only marking time.

Along the way we talked about how Stone Roses had paved the way for Bands such as Oasis and The Verve. At some stage Tabi let me know that her father had gone on his annual pilgrimage to Scotland, with the intention of drowning in Glenmorangie whisky.

So there we were, just the two of us, when we got back to the big stone house where she lived, and I found myself throwing my leather jacket across the dining table in the cavernous kitchen. Then she surprised me by taking a cigarette out of a twenty pack she had brought back with her in her handbag.

I was surprised because it wasn't the kind of thing I would have expected from Tabi. Cigarettes were not the thing among the smart set in my year. It wasn't even a spliff or anything. It was only a Marlboro – the first out of a virgin pack. I suppose I wondered what was going on.

'Can I ask you something?' she said, while she was making a mess of lighting her cigarette off the gas ring on their huge old range.

I thought, *Oh, shit!* I just don't fancy it when somebody starts a conversation off like that.

'You're so laid back. You just don't give a damn.' Her voice was slurred, but not all that slurred.

'What I am, Tabi, is stupid.'

'Oh, come on! You're only stupid in the way you want yourself to be stupid. I've been watching you, Mylie. Some of the girls have been talking about you.'

You have no idea how things like that irritate me. I hate it when other people, especially girls, talk about me.

'I mean – God! You don't care what anybody thinks about you.'

I couldn't be bothered to argue with her. I was still thinking about what she had just said, about talking about me with those other girls. I felt a wave of anger come up out of the pit of my stomach. I must have looked less than grateful, accepting a cigarette from this girl who didn't really smoke and taking a couple of drags, leaning my arm on the kitchen table.

'I wish I could understand somebody like you, Mylie,' she pushed it, squinting against the smoke. By now her perfume was all over the place. You couldn't escape it. And she has these big grey eyes that never seem to really look at you. They focus somewhere at the back of your head.

If she thought I was going to talk about myself with her, she didn't know me. I didn't say anything at all. The truth was I was getting twitchy. She had found a Ray Charles CD that belonged to her father, and while I was seeing to the coffee we sat and smoked, listening to tracks like 'You Are My Sunshine' and 'I Can't Stop Loving You'. It would be hard to find any music of quality that I couldn't enjoy. Honestly – you'll find it difficult to believe that I wasn't all that suspicious, even then, but that's how stupid I can be. I made the coffee and I found some milk in the old boneshaker of a fridge.

'You know what some of us are thinking of doing?'

'What's that?' I slid the mug in front of her.

This was the time when miniskirts had come back into fashion, with splits up to their hips, and she was wearing one. The smoke was making her eyes water so her eye makeup was starting to spread out over her face, like spiders' webs. She had taken to half leaning on the table very close to me, so her right breast was pressing against my arm.

'Wouldn't you love to take a year off after A-levels?' she asked me. 'A group of us are planning to chill out for a while before university. We thought we could buy a minibus cheap in Australia and do it up for a laugh and drive all over the Nullarbor Plain.' She laughed. Tabi has a delicious low-pitched kind of laugh. 'You don't need to look at me like that.'

Of course I knew she would never go to Australia, but I didn't tell her that. What I was thinking was that I wouldn't have minded getting lost in the desert of Australia with her myself. Drinking beer and getting laid every night wouldn't be half bad.

Tabi was saying, 'I really hate even thinking about going straight to university after this. I know I'm going to have to work like hell to get the grades I need.'

I wondered why she was talking like this. You don't know her – I mean, you don't know the image she had, up to this point, projected into the world. I was thinking that I wouldn't have minded going to university if they had some course that I was really interested in. Psychology hadn't yet occurred to me, although it interests me now. I think now that I might be happy studying psychology. I could get a kick out of sitting around just thinking about the mind and all that. Janus doesn't half mock me when I say things like that to him. He says, 'You should be hung up by the bollocks, old boy, to get the circulation back to your brains!'

I suppose I was shaking my head or something because Tabi suddenly started crying. I mean, weeping real tears.

She was saying something to the effect of: 'Oh, shit, shit – shit! Don't listen to me, Mylie. I'm drunk.'

I couldn't believe that she was as drunk as she was making out. I was taking careful swigs of my coffee to hide the fact I was getting horny from the way she was looking at me. Women know how to do that out of instinct. I just couldn't help myself. I reached out and brushed one of those tears that were running down her face.

So that was how we ended up climbing the stairs to her bedroom.

She never told me she planned it but later on I realised that she had. I should have suspected it there and then, and maybe I did too and didn't mind. Maybe it flattered me that this middle-class girl with the nice clothes and the long brown hair was lusting after me.

7

'Hello, Gorgeous!' Mary growled at me, as I was wheeling the laundry down the ward.

Mary is Lesley's friend. These are our escapologists, a couple of people who have been coming in and out of Constable ward for years. Lesley is little and thin with mousey brown hair cut like a boy's and Mary looks like Desperate Dan. This is one of the surprising things about the people here: they wear their minds on the outside. You get to know them a lot better than anybody you meet in ordinary life, better even than you know your own family and friends.

Lesley is twenty-eight years old. She's one of those people who eat things because of their illness. You are not going to believe it when I tell you that Lesley will even eat light bulbs. I'm not joking.

Lesley, like Harry, is a 'DSH', which means that she does things to herself that cause deliberate self-harm. She does this because she was sexually abused when she was a child. Lesley is the gentlest person I have ever met but she has a fragile sense of her own reality.

We have about twenty of these young women who are all DSHs and every one of them has been sexually abused. It's absolutely tragic.

You would recognise them straight away because they all look about thirteen years old. This is because they dress like children. They sit around all day curled up into themselves, like kids who have just had the hiding of their lives. As you might imagine, they're really damaged people. They can't live a normal life. They abuse themselves all the time. Their arms are all slashed with scars from glass or razor blades. Some of them have scars across their throats. All of them have taken countless drug overdoses.

To prevent them doing this, the doctors have an arrangement whereby they let them come into the ward for a limited period every month - something we call 'respite care'. The consultants, like Doctor Mehta and Doctor Boyson, will offer them this as a way of supporting them when they leave the Unit. I have even heard Doctor Boyson put it to Lesley in a way that is ponderously obvious.

He said to her, 'I'll let you come in four days a month, Lesley, provided you promise me that when you go home you won't harm yourself.'

So Lesley has made that bargain with Doctor Boyson about her good behaviour.

He has also worked out a strategy of treatment for her that is aimed at helping her regain her self-confidence. You are beginning to see why they take so much trouble to make the Unit look more like home, with the staff all dressed and acting like friends who care about you.

The problem with people like Lesley is that when it comes to the time to leave the Unit, they don't want to go home – not to those flooded burrows down in the ground.

Lesley isn't content just to be on the ward. She likes to be on Constant Nursing Observations. When a patient is on 'CNOs' there has to be a nurse or Health Care Assistant with her twenty-four hours a day. All day yesterday the nurses were doing their best to try to stop Lesley getting herself put on CNOs because it gives them extra work to do.

This week I am back working on earlies. The first thing I knew about it was when Barry, the charge nurse on Constable, called me into his office about eight o'clock to tell me. He said that he wanted me to keep an eye on Lesley. They had had to call out the SHO during the night because she had swallowed a load of drawing pins.

Lesley had gone around the wards taking the drawing pins out of the notice boards, but she hadn't swallowed them all because she didn't want the posters to fall down.

Everybody just assumed that what she would have done was to bend the spiky bit flat. That's what she's done in the past. But this time she had left all the spiky bits sticking out. They had just got the X-rays back when I got to the office and Barry showed me the drawing pins. I'm talking about dozens of them, in her stomach with the spiky bits sticking out. She had also swallowed three sewing needles, which she must have nicked from OT - big sewing needles, about two to three inches long. I could see the eyes of the needles very clearly on the X-rays. They had still refused to put her on CNOs by the time it came to early morning but then she swallowed one of the light bulbs. Of course she didn't just swallow it whole. She isn't an ostrich. What she did was to take a bulb out of one of the bedside wall-lights and smash it on top of her locker and swallow the broken glass. She was careful to scoop up every piece of broken glass and swallow it, so that nobody else would cut themselves on it.

She won that one.

Lesley got herself put on CNOs. And that means she has had to be put in the Safe Room.

So Mary was left without her best friend. Mary can be a bit of a pest when that happens. She's about forty and a lot bigger than most men. It's fortunate for people such as me, who have to look after her, that she's so gentle.

She first came to her doctor's attention when she said that children were following her around the streets, hitting her and calling her names. You can imagine they would because she looks absolutely bizarre. She wears her hair hanging all the way down her back, a kind of mazy auburn hair with a lot of grey in it. It's long and straggly and she ties it together in a single plait. She has a crimped fringe that starts halfway back on her head and sweeps forward over her eyes to hide the fact that she's balding. It sticks out several inches in front of her face like the peak of a baseball cap, only much thicker, more like a ski-slope than the peak of a cap. And then she has glasses and huge dangly earrings. Tons of necklaces all different colours. She wears brightly-coloured clothes and the colours clash. She also wears a red and yellow and green top. She came back into the Unit this time when the police found her in a telephone box shouting and beating up somebody who wasn't there.

The strange thing about Mary is that she's actually a man. She's a massive, awkward-looking man who thinks he's a woman. We have accepted that Mary should be regarded as a woman because she really does act and think like a woman. In fact she believes she's the most beautiful woman in the world. I sympathise with her because she has to shave twice a day. When she's really upset, like when Lesley is bad, she doesn't bother with shaving her chin. She fancies all the male nurses and doctors and they hate it.

Mary has developed quite a crush on me. She wanted somebody to take her to see *Cabaret* and so the nurses told her I was the only one who could take her into the West End.

So now she says, 'Hello, Gorgeous!' in this deep, growly voice, every time I see her.

It's a bit of a pain, but I don't mind.

Mary is the ringleader, always trying to escape from the ward. She pretends to be getting better so that she can get away from observations and then she makes a run for it.

When she first came back this time under a compulsory detention order she was trying to escape every thirty seconds. That was a real drag because the wards aren't locked. The doctors think it's important that the patients know that the wards are never locked. Even the Safe Room is only locked when it absolutely needs to be.

Poor old Mary never gets very far. Sometimes she makes it out into the garden, or even as far as the car park, but somebody always catches up with her and brings her back to us.

Once I asked Mary why the children were following her and she said to me, 'It's because I'm so beautiful.'

The reason Mary thinks these things is she is also suffering from schizophrenia. She hears the voices of these children following her about and even when she's on the first floor ward she thinks they're knocking on her window because they're jealous of the fact that she's so beautiful. The nurses don't want Doctor Mehta to treat this delusion. They think it's a really lovely delusion because Mary is pleased with herself all the time. So the nurses tell her that the doctor is pleased with her and she comes up to me with a big smile on her face and she says to me, 'Doctor Mehta is very pleased with me.'

That's the wonderful thing about Mary: she's always smiling.

Let me tell you, it isn't just the patients who are worth studying. The staff are all sleeping with one another. They have to keep moving wards as they fall out with each other. It's really hilarious.

I've already told you about the gorgeous tanned five feet eight blonde-haired blue-eyed Anna on reception, who doesn't half give me the horn. The thing that counts against me with gorgeous Anna is the fact I'm only nineteen years old. I complain it isn't fair and keep dropping the hint that I'm nearly twenty. I'll be twenty this coming September.

A lot of the nurses are married men but Anna still works through them at the rate of a new one every two months. Everybody knows about it. Anybody on the ward could give you the list in the right order. She's actually an incredibly nice person, not bitchy to the other women or anything. She once told me a story about when she was eating at a pavement restaurant in Soho and one of the Italian waiters annoyed every other customer because he gathered up the roses off all the tables and made a bouquet of them so he could go down on one knee and propose to her.

Anyway, by the time it got to the tea break, I decided I would call in and say hello to Harry.

These days I often call in to spend a few minutes with Harry.

Harry and I have got over our differences about Sheffield and my Irish name. Not, I suppose, that Harry ever gave a damn really. I just think he deserves to have somebody call in and see him since his wife hasn't been in to see him at all in what is now three weeks since he was first admitted. It isn't easy to get the time because the wards are short staffed and they have me running around like a train. But I think I should keep an eye on him because he isn't doing so very well.

He's suffering from a severe depression. Only Grumpy doesn't call it depression, he calls it melancholia. That's some term, *melancholia*. I like the sound of it better than common-or-garden depression.

Grumpy is a little bit puzzled about Harry. He hasn't been able to find any definite reason why this melancholia should have come over him. Often when somebody gets really down there's a very obvious reason for it. The psychiatrists will try to winkle this out because if they can put the cause right the patient is more likely to get better.

The problem is that some people get depressed for no reason at all. Grumpy knows that Harry does have one or two physical problems to worry about. He has a kind of diabetes that is treated with pills and he has a cancer of the prostate. Of course Grumpy has looked into that – but it seems that the cancer is no big problem. I mean, it isn't slowly eating away at him like you would expect of a cancer. His cancer is keeping itself to itself. In fact the biggest physical problem Harry has to suffer is that pain he still suffers in his right arm and shoulder from an old attack of shingles.

It's the weirdest pain you ever saw. One minute he'll be sitting there, quiet in his chair. And the next thing he'll be screwing his body over to his right, almost touching the ground, groaning, 'Oh, the pain! The pain!'

One thing I have discovered about Harry is the reason he was swearing so much when he first came in.

Harry is an old soldier. He was once an army officer, a major. He didn't mention it to Grumpy during the interview, so, for some reason, he must have decided to keep quiet about it. When you work in a place like the Unit, you wonder about things that people leave out. All the same, now that we know about it, it's really obvious. It isn't just the swearing or the sort of clipped way he talks. You'd spot it straight away from the way he swings his arms when he walks.

'Hello, Harry!' I say to him, sitting on the bed next to his armchair so I can talk to him.

Harry doesn't even look at me.

I like to hear him talk, because Harry has an interesting kind of voice. Actually, now that I know he was a major in the army, I can see his voice fits him like his bowler hat.

'My grandad', I continue, 'was a soldier in the North Africa campaign. I just wondered if you could have been in Montgomery's army. That would mean you could have been fighting in the same battles.'

Harry still doesn't say anything, but I can tell he's listening.

'I don't know. I mean, I'm not even sure you're old enough to have fought in the Second World War.'

Of course I know he's old enough. I am just trying to get a reaction. But it's no good. He just won't talk about it at all. Old Harry is still down there at the bottom of his well.

Sometimes I talk to Harry about my friends, Janus and Rich. He doesn't really have much to say. Today I go on to tell him a little bit about Tabi, which he listens to with his right shoulder down and his head turned towards the window. You don't need to tell me that this is a really stupid thing to do. I mean, why the hell do I have to do a thing like that after Tabi and I haven't even seen each other for so long? I have decided that I'm never going to repeat that mistake.

But I hate it when Harry sits there in his chair with his head turned towards the window all the time. It's the *way* he looks towards the window. I know what he's thinking when he keeps looking towards the window. There's nothing to see because it is dark outside.

I'm not saying that Harry has altogether deteriorated. There are some aspects to his melancholy that have improved.

For one thing, he doesn't have those rages any more. But you can never take anything for granted. I have seen other patients who seem to get better very quickly but all the time they're playing tricks with you and as soon as they get home they top themselves.

It upsets me to have to leave him looking like that and so I start telling him more about Tabi than I planned to. It just slips out, to be honest with you. Anyway, I end up talking about the fact that her father comes from Scotland and the fact that she is into dancing.

'Dancing,' he mutters. It is the first word he has spoken to me in nearly a week and it comes out in this croaky voice. His voice has dropped so low I have to listen carefully to tell that he is saying anything at all.

It's the fact he has spoken this single word that makes me go into it more than I should, telling him how things ended up in a pathetic way between us and how she came down to London to get away from me.

'To get away from you,' he echoes.

That's one of the things people do when they're not well. They copy the words you say to them. It's enough to get on your nerves at times but you just have to be patient with people like Harry.

Hey, but now I am really going to town, telling him all about the way things just didn't work out between us in the end.

Can you believe that I'm doing a stupid thing like that?

It seems to interest him because his head comes around and he has a little spell of groaning under his breath, but then he fixes me with that fierce glare out of his clear blue eyes.

'Young man,' he says. It kills me the way he says that. 'It's no good asking my advice about women.'

Well, that started me laughing all right. It looks to me as if Harry and I have that same problem when it comes to women.

8

Today turned out to be a free Saturday, my first hard-earned weekend off this month, in between finishing on earlies and starting the despised lates again. So, in spite of the fact it was raining down in buckets, I intended to enjoy it.

The first thing I did when I got the job and the agency found me this place to live, was to go out and buy a brand new stack. I put myself into hock for two years to buy the best kit of separates I could afford. I started with a Marantz CD-63 MKII KI Signature, which puts out voices like silver magic and has a monumental bass that is positively scary. I put it together with a pioneer A-605R amp and Tannoy Profile speakers, saving a little money on a still excellent Yamaha KX-390 tape deck and Rega Planar record player.

So after a lunchtime breakfast, I didn't care that it was raining. I loaded Bob Marley's *Legend* CD and I lay on my bed and soaked it up, with a bottle of Bud Ice perched on my sternum, and I thought about Harry.

There is something very interesting about Harry.

It isn't at all unusual for patients to be brought in by the police as CDOs. It isn't even unusual for them to refuse to talk to us at first. Most of these patients are schizophrenics and they don't even know they're ill, so the admission comes as a bit of a shock to the system. But after a few days on treatment the delusions and the voices settle down inside their heads and they come round and start to make some kind of sense.

Harry appears to be different. I've been calling in to see him off and on and I have the impression he is not trying to get better.

So it was Harry, mainly, that I was thinking about while I was lying on my bed under the black and white poster of Bob and drinking iced beer and listening to 'No Woman No Cry', the live version from the London Lyceum concert.

I could see him really clearly in my mind. Harry. The way he just sits there quietly brooding, or sometimes reading his book. That book seems to be a very important thing to Harry. He treats it like his bible. I was beginning to wish that I had read Arthur Koestler's *Darkness At Noon*. It was only my gut instinct, but I had a feeling that the book might open up the doors to understanding Harry.

Then I thought to myself, *Ah, to hell with it!* I mean, I was feeling so incredibly laid back. There was that warm feeling sinking deeper and deeper into my soul as I drank the beer and let the music take me. I unscrewed a second bottle just to make a point of not thinking about it so much.

But it was no use. I was still feeling so damned good about myself that it seemed the most natural thing in the world to go out and buy the book.

I put on my black leather trench coat and I legged it through the rain to the underground station at Marble Arch, where I took the Central Line eastbound. I realised it was a mistake as soon as I re-emerged into the light on the Tottenham Court Road, because the traffic was atrocious. It was mid Saturday afternoon and still raining down in buckets. A black Mercedes limousine tried to take my legs off while I was making a dash for it across St Giles Circle.

'Ya bloody lunatic!' I shouted at the driver. But he didn't notice me through his tinted windows.

I found a Waterstone's on the Charing Cross Road, with a poster in the window announcing a signing by Doctor Boyson of his book, *Choices*. It really shook me to see his face, with its groomed white hair, staring out at me. There was a steady stream of late afternoon shoppers going into the shop and I joined them, heading down the wall of shelves labelled 'fiction', and looking for the 'Ks'. I found a copy of Koestler's book, a paperback priced at £6.99. But it looked very different from the book Harry was reading.

Harry's cover is positively evil. This was neat and shiny, a surreal montage of a phrenology head and an eye peering out of the face of a clock. I wandered to the counter, undecided. I was still deliberating at the till, with a queue of impatient customers building up behind me and the girl on the till already red-faced. So I handed her a tenner and pocketed my change before leaving the shop with the book, in a plastic bag, dangling from my hand.

I needed to get back to the opposite side of the road. I was about thirty yards away from the lights and doing my best to negotiate some stationary traffic when a cyclist in a red tracksuit ran straight into me from behind. I felt the blow and I tripped over the front wheel of her bike and fell down into the road. I felt absolutely stupid, caught out there in the middle of the impatient traffic. And there was a pain starting up in my wrist.

'Why don't you watch where you're going?' she said to me as I was struggling back on to my feet.

I couldn't believe that she was blaming me. I was so taken by surprise I didn't know what I was doing. I was rubbing my arm and looking under the wheels of the cars, where my book had fallen down next to the railings.

Then a busker came out of nowhere and helped me get back on to the safety of the pavement. I was covered in crap down the sleeve of my coat, but at least it wasn't torn.

'I saw what happened, mate, and it wasn't your fault,' the busker said, glaring at the disappearing cyclist. 'She was dodging and weaving between the taxis.' He somehow managed to rescue my book, which had fallen out of the plastic bag. The thing was half ruined because about half a dozen vehicles had rolled right over it.

'One of 'em tried to take off my legs,' I groaned. I was getting really mad by now, clenching my fists as he took me over to his doorway.

'You're nawt from Landin,' he observed, wiping the book down on his sleeve.

'Nah – from Sheffield.' By now I was also grinding my teeth.

I noticed that he was shivering. He was obviously on withdrawal from something pretty potent. He had been playing a saxophone in his doorway here on the corner.

'Sheffield!' he said, offering me a sip of his vodka. 'Two footbowl teams. When wahn goes up the other goes dahn.'

'Yeah!' I muttered. I was rubbing my wrist and shaking my head at the vodka because he looked as if he needed it more than I did. I added the three pound coins from my change to the collection in his cap.

'Fanks, mate,' he waved, taking a swig himself from the bottle. Then he started shouting after me, 'I see it oll the tahm. Those drivers – they're fahkin' animals.'

I found myself back on the edge of the Charing Cross Road, glaring at the traffic, smelling the fumes, my ears hurting from the squeal of brakes, the blaring of some distant horns. By now the plastic bag that had wrapped up the book was still further out into the road, where it was being chewed up by every passing car.

9

It was just past eight in the evening, a little congested because people were coming out of the common room after *Coronation Street* and heading in a chatty little cavalcade up to the Smoke Room.

Jock "the Heron" was pacing up and down, his bulging eyes frantic in his skull-like head, which was jerking forwards and backwards on his horizontal neck. Jock likes to prowl the corridors, with his shoulders bent and his head pushed out before him, talking away to himself in a whisper. But he was held up by the same obstruction that was stopping me getting past with Freda. I had to help her out of the wheelchair and hold her hand as she threaded her footsteps over the legs of Ursula, who was straddling the doorway on the landing on Gerries, thinking she was a gate.

William Blake is in a very artistic mood at the moment and Ursula is one of the actors. She suffers from a condition of waxy flexibility that causes her to make kinetic statements from her body postures.

Then Freda had to say goodbye to Donald, our manic-depressive dressed in baggy cream cords and a string vest. Donald, who exhibits pictures at the Royal Academy when he is well, was drawing one of his fantastically detailed graveyard scenes in red and black crayons on the flipchart near to the nurses' station. Donald wanted to hug Freda. While he was removing his unlit cigar from his mouth and his Panama hat from his head, I listened to Alice, the Jamaican nursing assistant, singing Ursula back on to her feet so she could go back to her bed and pose in comfort.

'You'll miss us, won't you, Freda?' I asked her, wheeling her towards the lift.

'Yes, I will, Mylie,' she said.

We went out through the reception area to get to the main corridor. Here I turned left, so I could take Freda out through the direct exit from the Unit, which opens off an L-shaped corridor on to a tarmac path that runs between rose gardens. Our breath came out in white clouds that trailed us through the icy air. Freda suddenly shoved her right hand out to the side, as if she wanted to touch the roses, which were looking different shades of orange in the electric light.

She called out, in an amazed voice, 'Oh, look – there's almost a full moon.'

'Come on, Freda,' I said to her. 'Don't tell me you've never seen the moon before.'

'I haven't seen it look so lovely,' she laughed, and her laughter was so contagious that I stopped pushing her for a few moments to look up at it.

'Hey, Freda,' I laughed, 'if only I were fifty years older!'

To be honest, I was remembering little Freda, with her almost-bald head, stiff as a statue, coming down for ECT. It was great to see her so much better. I took a deep breath of the icy air, which smelled of nothing but freshness in my nostrils. Freda's two daughters, themselves grey-haired, were waiting by a silver Renault Clio, with the back door open to spill its light out into the falling dark. Freda and I had come to a secret understanding. I put on the brakes and helped her out of the chair when we were still ten feet away so she could walk to the car. Freda wanted to walk on her own.

Her daughters were embarrassed by my presence but they clucked around Freda, wrapping a scarf around her neck so they didn't have to look at the scar on her throat. Then each of them took an arm to help her into the car. I thought it was nice to see her two daughters fussing around her like that but Freda had other ideas. She scolded them in a piping voice. 'You don't need to treat me like an invalid,' she said. 'I can manage very well for myself, thank you.'

I was biting the tip of my tongue to stop myself laughing.

She stopped when she was halfway through the car door, turned her head to the side to look at me and said to one of her daughters, 'This is Mylie.' She turned to wink at me. 'I've been telling him all about you.'

That, of course, was really wicked.

'Just make sure you arrange for the gas bills to be paid by standing order in future,' I said, with a playful wave of my fist.

But it only seemed to increase the daughters' embarrassment as they closed the door of the car behind her.

They were the reason she was leaving the Unit so late in the evening. One of them lived in Stratford and could only get down to London after work. Michael had talked them into an arrangement: Freda would only be living in her own home for two weeks out of every month. Each daughter would take it in turns to have Freda in her home for one week. That was why they both had to be present, since neither seemed to trust the other. They didn't say a word to me, not even thank you, before driving away.

I thought I might have caught a single small wave, Freda blowing me a kiss out of the back window of the car.

On my way back to Gerries, I looked up at the second floor and I saw Harry. He was standing there, looking out of his window. It made me realise that Harry had come into the Unit just two weeks after Freda, and she had been a damn sight more depressed than he was. Yet here was old Freda on her way home and all Harry could do was look down at it happening from his window.

I knock on the door, as usual, before entering the side ward. Harry hasn't moved from his place by the window. He is wearing a white shirt, with a dribble stain down the front, and grey hospital trousers over blue and brown tartan hospital-issue slippers.

I can smell him when I get up close. There's a smell about patients when they are really down. I can smell that smell, mixed with a linament he rubs around his shoulder and under his arm. He has what I would call a pouchy face.

There is a second face, made up of muscle underneath – you can tell that in his prime Harry must have had a really strong, muscular kind of a face – only now the muscles seem to clench away there between his jaws independently of the loose skin of his face. Sometimes I get the impression that underneath the pouchy skin there is a different Harry, in the bones and the sinews and muscles, trapped in there under the old skin. But I don't want to give you the wrong idea about Harry or the way he looks. He has a strong face, a very expressive face. Not too many lines so there is something slightly moonish about it, and a look in his eyes of vagueness, of infinite distance. I know that I must try to drag his eyes back out of that infinite distance to get him to focus on me, so he will really talk to me.

I say, 'Hello, Harry.' My voice seems to echo around the room.

There is a sound from him, nothing more than a grunt.

There is a strange feeling entering Harry's room. It's different from all of the others in that there is nothing personal in it. No flowers, no cards wishing him to get well, no photographs, not even a newspaper thrown on the bed. I suppose the only ornaments in Harry's room are the curtains, which are a single tone of blue, two shades darker than his eyes.

I get up close to him. I am standing next to him. I tower over him really. He isn't tall to start with and he seems to be shrinking into himself.

I glance out of the window and try to imagine what he would have seen. Me wheeling Freda along through the flower beds. Freda's balding head, reflecting the orange light. Her hand reaching out towards the roses, her face turning upwards, one moon looking at another.

'Why do you watch the car park all the time?'

'No reason,' he says.

'You must be looking for some reason.'

He maintains his silence, irritated at my intrusion but still standing there, slightly hunched about his shoulders, looking down in the direction of the car-park. Of course he doesn't look me in the eyes.

'A man has been coming in here,' he murmurs, 'asking me for money.'

'What does he look like? Does he looks like this?' I imitate a mean and half-crazy face with dewlap cheeks, making barping sounds every few seconds.

Harry looks at me a moment, assessing, before replying. 'Comes right up to me. Stares me in the face. The same thing, over and over. "I want my money. Give me my money!"'

'It's only old Barney Silkes. If he's really upsetting you, I'll have a word with Michael.'

Harry sighs. 'I have no money to give him.' He shakes his head. 'I've had no money for weeks on end now. No money to spend on anything.'

'Have you asked the nurses? They have a safe on the ward, for small amounts.'

'They wouldn't give it to you, unless... unless your situation was different. I haven't a penny to go out, even if I wanted to – even if I was able to. I couldn't buy a paper. I couldn't buy blades for my razor. Not even a packet of cigarettes. When I could kill for a smoke.'

I hesitate, because I detect a calculating intelligence beneath the surface confusion.

'Maybe they're just worried that your memory is confused by the medication. You might put the money down somewhere and forget about it.'

'No. No – I'm not quite that bad. For seventy per cent of the time, I may have been a bit muggy. What do you call it ...?'

'Forgetful?'

'Yes - forgetful. For seventy per cent of the time I have spent here, I have had a bit of a problem. Nothing serious. Just something I had to look at myself and think, "Well – you had better just carry on anyway!"'

'You seem a little better to me,' I say encouragingly, giving him a pound coin, which he accepts with a sideways glance at my boots before he tucks it into his grey hospital-issue trousers pocket. 'Soon you'll be able to walk around. You'll be able to go to the Smoke Room and damage your lungs to your heart's content. But you've got to cooperate with Vera and go and get back into things. Join the others in OT.'

I know that Harry has been saying no to occupational therapy.

No reaction.

'You can't just go saying no to things that might help you to get better.'

'And then you'll come along and take me out for a drink?'

I have to laugh. There is a sense of humour in there, somewhere down in the deep dark well, below the blue membranes of his eyes.

I feel oddly nervous about what I am about to say. I've been working towards it, picking my moment. This has to be the moment. I can't help the way my voice falls so it's just a husky whisper. I say to Harry, 'Do you want to talk? I mean, do you want to talk about what's upsetting you?'

No response. Nothing. For a moment I think he hasn't heard me, but then I notice that he isn't breathing.

There is a horrible silence that seems to chill the room. It's more than just a silence, it's a stillness that congeals like ice on my skin. But then I hear him breathing again.

He is breathing slowly, noisily. There is a whistling sound as he inhales breath through his nose. I can smell that smell about him, even stronger. I see the way his hand is trembling, the hand that is holding the book.

He mumbles, so low I can't make it out.

'What did you say?' I'm feeling pretty uncomfortable in this terrible atmosphere that has continued over from the silence.

'I said', he squeezes the words out bitterly, furiously, through his teeth, 'that you have no right to... to ask me that.'

My head is shaking all of its own. I'm grinning a hopeless grin, feeling foolish. 'I'm sorry.'

I can hear how useless the apology sounds, echoing in the room. I assume that it's because the room is so bare of ornaments. A slightly odd effect, amplifying the deeper notes especially. Harry is quiet again, just standing there, trembling. That's all he is doing - staring out of the window, trembling. Those blue eyes, lost within themselves in the pouchy face with its bunched up muscles underneath. I notice the freckles on the dome of his head. His head is a beach of small pale freckles, freckles like stones in the pale white sand. I don't know why I haven't noticed them before.

'I didn't mean to upset you even more. I just thought that maybe you wanted to talk.'

The tension between us has reached such an unbearable intensity I feel jerky, slightly faint, as our eyes meet, but not in the flesh.

I am looking into the reflection of Harry's eyes in the window. The face in the reflection is whiter still but the eyes are not blue. They are black, all-black. It feels as if I am looking down into the bottomless pit of his melancholy, into the darkness that has taken hold of his soul.

Then he speaks in a voice I haven't heard him use before. It isn't his clipped army officer's voice. It's a much gentler voice, hardly above a murmur.

'What about you? Do you want to talk to me about yourself?'

'I don't mind. If that's what you want.'

'Well - go ahead then!'

'Yeah – well ...' The truth is I am thinking that this is a dirty trick that Harry is playing on me because I cannot think of a thing to say. I don't lead a very interesting life.

The sound of rain on the window. The rapping of fingers out there in the dark.

'Why', he demands, 'are you so eager to know about me?'

A hesitation on my part now. This conversation isn't going the way I had anticipated. A lot of patients just love to talk. They will tell you every secret of their lives without a second thought.

I say, 'Because I'm concerned about you.' Then I just shrug my shoulders and shake my head. 'Because I want to understand you.'

A further leap in the tension between us. Those black eyes no longer meeting mine. The head averted. The real eyes, the blue eyes, not daring even to turn around to look sideways into mine.

I talk about Freda. Harry must have come across Freda, since he has spent all this time on the same ward with her. Everybody meets everybody else on the wards. I talk about her going home. 'She's really happy about it,' I say. 'I think you saw her leave. Her relatives came to fetch her. Her two daughters.'

'Yes,' he mutters.

Of course he knows all this. He knows that I have seen him watching, from up here in his window.

'In time, you'll get better too. You'll go home.'

His left hand is rising slowly. It reaches his right shoulder and it begins to rub at it. The shoulder seems to writhe around under the touch of the hand, to twist within itself, beginning to move down. There is something wounding about the way this happens. Something that reaches out towards me and moves me profoundly. It is so uncontrollably unconscious.

'You live near here? In a flat in the hospital?'

I have told him half a dozen times where I live. I say, 'You remember, Harry, I live in Kensington, the house we call "The Palace", which I share with my friends.'

'With your friends ...' he echoes, as I watch the hand rubbing, massaging relentlessly.

'Yeah,' I nod. 'I've told you all about them. Janus, who is out of work. And Rich, who is a Crusty, with a ring through his nose.'

He's shaking his head, as if it's the first he's heard of them. It is the shock still. The reaction in him. I can feel it, smell it from the pores of his skin. I can taste it on my tongue.

'You get along with them, these ... these friends of yours?'

'We hit it off really well.' I'm talking again with my normal voice. I'm calmer now, maybe a little bit resentful. But I realise I have to be extra patient with him.

'I know what you do,' he says. 'You go out at night and you all get good and drunk together.'

I laugh to myself because he's got it right. He has hit that nail right on the head.

But old Harry is standing there with tears in his eyes. I reach out my hand to touch his good shoulder, but he will not accept the touch. He surprises me with the vigour with which he shrugs me off, the shock still unsettling him, the shock of intrusion, of discovering – I hope – that there is this door of communication that is just opening. I sense it too, in my own way. That's why I avoid mentioning Muriel, his wife, whom he tried to strangle.

'Out there ...' his voice is a little more forceful, as if in the rejection of my comforting him, he is rediscovering strengths within himself. 'You asked me that question.'

'That's right,' I say. 'I just wondered what you were looking at out there.'

'I'm looking at them.'

'But why? What's so interesting about them? People are just people.'

'No,' he says. 'Out there, those are people. In here, we are patients.'

10

When I got home I lay on my bed and I thought about things. Patients are amazing - the way he just said that. It really made me think about Harry, how he must feel like a prisoner on the ward. Yet the only thing that is keeping him prisoner is his own mind.

It is the mind that is truly amazing.

And that got me wondering about the fact that people like Doctor Boyson talk about how the mind is the metaphysical product of the brain.

Take Freda, for example. I recalled the way her brain was affected when Maggie passed the electricity through it. It was as if the disturbed programming in her mind had been wiped clear by a bolt of lightning. It makes you wonder if the brain really is like a computer, as Dr Boyson is always telling us.

I am very interested in the human mind. I have been thinking quite a lot about it since I started work on the Unit. For example, we all know that the mind is the expression of the brain. If you had no brain, you wouldn't be able to think at all. So the mind has to be the product of the brain. But anybody with any kind of a brain knows that your mind is a lot more complicated than you would expect a computer to be. When you really think about it, when you lie back and think about the human imagination, the way we have harnessed the power of the atom, our ability to create music for example – the way we *feel*. There are people who still think that we feel through our hearts but that's just bullshit. We feel through our minds, we love and care for people through our minds. We even hate people and do terrible things, all through the perversion of our minds.

That's what makes it so hard to believe that the brain is just a computer. Would a computer make doctors want to cure diseases or Picasso paint or Mozart write music? Would it take us to the moon?

So then you find yourself thinking about it in a whole different kind of a way. You begin to wonder if Grumpy is closer. I have no doubt that he believes in the notion of an old-fashioned God. And that makes me wonder where he thinks the soul might be – for example, if he thinks that the soul is another way of talking about the mind.

So you see the kind of territory you get into when you start thinking about psychiatry.

To me it means that when the mind is sick in some way, disturbed to the extent that we see in our patients on the Unit, it is all the more interesting than a physical illness, such as a heart attack or a cancer.

11

'Well, this woman, now... this woman... I would say that she is a very shrewd person.'

I was getting to know Harry. Recognising his need to come up for air, to rise out of the darkness of his well and into what must still appear to him a kind of twilight.

'What woman are we talking about, Harry?'

'This woman... this woman, who came to talk to me.'

I shrugged my shoulders, to show Harry we had the time. To reassure him there was no need to hurry. 'What was she like? Describe her to me.'

Harry described a tall young woman, with fair hair tied up on to the back of her head. 'I was able to smell her perfume,' he said.

'Ah!'

'Yes – her perfume.' That slow blink of his eyes. The struggle for concentration, the two deep lines biting deeply into his brow between his eyes. 'I don't remember her name.'

'When did she come to see you?'

'Today. She came to see me today.' His eyes were suddenly brightening. His head was becoming erect. 'It seemed to be important.'

I nodded. I was perched once more on the edge of his bed and he was sitting in his chair. 'What did she ask you about?'

The pause was shorter.

'Personal things. Concerning myself and Muriel.'

There was only one woman on the unit whose perfume Harry would have noticed and who would have asked Harry in a professional way about Muriel: Claudia, the social worker. Claudia, with the Sloane Ranger voice, who was currently being serviced by Lane 'Choices' Boyson.

I had forgotten to ask Harry the brand he smoked, so I had bought him twenty Benson and Hedges. Now I handed the pack over to him. I explained that there was an official ban against smoking in any of the ward sleeping areas, including side wards, but he could enjoy them to his heart's content down the corridor in the Smoke Room. Then, after a slight hesitation – reassuring myself that Harry was not going to set fire to himself – I handed him the small box of red-top matches.

'Is Muriel coming to see you?'

He looked down at the cigarettes and then shoved the packet deep into his trousers pocket. 'I don't know.'

'But this woman, the social worker, is going to go and see her for you?'

'I think so. I hope so.' His eyes moved around to regard me, giving me that furtive sideways look. 'I said to her, "Could I go out, perhaps at the weekend, and see Muriel for myself?" I promised her I would be no bother. No problem.'

'I'm sure Claudia will look into that for you.'

'Do you think so?'

'Yes, I do.'

Harry spent a few seconds considering that, sitting quietly in his chair. It was great to see how he was looking a shade brighter, his skin a better colour, a little less puffy and white.

'I'm not getting my hopes too high. I'm not expecting to go out soon.'

'You'll go home, all right. Don't you worry.'

He lifted his head and looked at me, another of his sideways glances. There is an incredible shyness in those glances of Harry's, like a timid little creature poking its head out of its burrow into an uncertain landscape. I noticed that the book wasn't on his locker, so he must have hidden it away somewhere, perhaps in the drawer underneath.

'I'd be most grateful if that could be done. The people here don't talk to me. I have been going out into the corridor. There are all these men and women about the place, sitting around or talking to themselves. They don't talk sense at all. They don't talk back to me.'

'Does this upset you?'

'I can't stand it.'

'I can imagine that. It must be really frustrating.'

'Loneliness is a killer. Now that I have lost my family, it's a terrible thing.'

That didn't make sense to me. I didn't think of Muriel as a family as such. It was the first time that Harry had ever mentioned his family to me and I waited to see if he would say any more. But he said nothing.

I was careful not to put him off. I kept myself still, just sitting there, having a sip of my tea. 'Would you like to talk about it - about Muriel?'

'No,' he said, 'I would not.'

He wasn't looking at me. His eyes were moving here and there - the window, the blue curtains. Eyes that had become something other than eyes. Eyes that had become unseeing. He hadn't put down the matches. Instead his right hand played around with them bemusedly, twirling the box on his lap.

'She's your wife after all,' I prompted. 'And she hasn't been coming in to see you.'

'No,' he said.

'I think that's a bit much. Not coming in even once to see you.'

A small hesitation. 'You can't blame Muriel.'

'Well, I can see that she might be feeling very angry with you after what you tried to do to her.'

A longer hesitation. His voice low, hardly a human sound at all, the sound of a breeze through dried-up autumn leaves. 'No – no, it isn't that. There are other things. Muriel was good to me. I was the one who did it. It was my fault.'

'What is happening between you and Muriel is very sad,' I murmured, shifting slightly.

'No, you don't understand. Muriel is not my wife.'

'Not your wife?'

'My wife, my real wife, Elizabeth, is living in Australia.'

'Your real wife?'

'Yes. With my son, Teddy.'

I had to edge my feet around on the floor. The thing is, people like Harry can get confused. They think that what they have been dreaming about, their delusions, are real.

'You didn't tell Dr Dury about that.'

'No.' A little agitatedly.

I still wasn't sure if I believed him. 'You can't just go not telling the doctors things when they're trying to help you.'

'I don't have to tell them everything.'

'Yes, you do. If you want to get better.'

'I'd rather you didn't tell anybody else.'

'Don't talk daft!'

'Do you hear me now? Not a word. I want your word on that.'

Now I was the one who had to come up for air. I believed him. He seemed too intense to be anything other than factual about it.

'I can't promise you that, Harry.'

Suddenly there was ice in his voice. His face was the officer's face, hard and as cold as marble. 'You must give me your word, son.'

'Okay.' Though I didn't know if I could honestly keep it. 'So who is Muriel then?'

'Muriel is the woman I have lived with for twenty-seven years.'

I thought, *twenty-seven years.*

'Well,' I said, choosing my words, 'it's not so unusual these days.'

'I know. It's a bit of a mess.'

'It's not such a big deal. These things happen to a lot of people.'

'I feel so ashamed about it.'

I sensed something more. Something Harry was not telling me. I was watching that hand twirling the matches round and round. Watching his head falling. I had to get him away from this subject, which was obviously very painful to him.

'I've tried reading your book. I went out and bought a copy for myself.'

'You've been reading *Darkness at Noon*?'

'Well - I'm only part way through. I haven't managed to finish it yet.'

'Why? Why are you reading it?'

'I think I might be able to understand what you see in it. I mean, there's a feeling you might be glimpsing something - how can I put it? Like you're looking down through the surface of the ocean and you catch a flash of something really deep and terrifying.'

He screwed up his eyes, shook his head. Opened his eyes again, blinking into the light, but he seemed unable to look at me directly.

'It's okay if you don't want to talk about it.'

'No. It's just difficult for me to find the words.' Still shaking his head, his eyes blinking more slowly, his eyes lost in their distance. 'It's not so much what I see in it. Not seeing...'

'What then? Searching?'

'I don't know.'

'I would imagine', I encouraged him, 'that it's the sort of book that you pick up and read and you can tell from the very beginning that you are learning something new about people.'

'Perhaps that's it,' he replied.

But it wasn't a very convincing performance. There was something more, something he wouldn't or couldn't tell me. Restlessly, I shifted my feet again, resisted the urge to stand up – do something, anything, to break the tension.

Then he spoke more softly still, addressing his words to somewhere else, somewhere deep and secretly internal, as if curling into himself. 'With you, must I pay for ever for righteous acts? Did the righteous man perhaps carry the heaviest debt?'

His words sounded like a psalm or a prayer, but I knew, although I didn't recognise them, that they were words he remembered from *Darkness at Noon*.

He had surprised me again. I didn't know what to say for a moment or two. I was thinking back to that time when I had interrupted him in a dream, or a nightmare, when he had tried to jump up out of his chair with his right fist clenched.

'Who was R. Giles?'

Suddenly Harry was tensing, his reluctance showing. 'Somebody who recommended the book to me.'

'And you kept it ? His copy?'

'I suppose I did.' Hostile now. Wary.

'Why?'

He inhaled, stiffening, and there was that musical sound from the narrowing inside one of his nostrils. A flush invading the beach of his head, like a tide washing around the pebbly freckles. 'It was such a long time ago.'

'During the war?'

His eyes came over then and he looked at me, eye to eye. There was that fierce brilliance of anger in his eyes again. The hydrogen flames. He said nothing.

'He died, didn't he? This R. Giles, who lent you his book.'

Harry's face had turned to stone. He didn't shake his head or even so much as nod.

'He was one of your friends? Another soldier?'

'He was... an officer in my regiment. He wasn't very much older than I was.'

That hesitation before Harry called him an officer. It seemed significant, although I couldn't imagine what its significance was. 'How old were you?'

'Twenty. I was twenty years old. He was five years older than me.'

'He died though, didn't he?'

'A lot of people died.'

'Do you want to talk about it? You don't have to, if it's too painful for you.'

He glanced at me and smiled again. 'The army ran in my family. My father fought on the Somme and at Ypres in the First War.'

'Was that why you became a soldier?'

'Everybody who was able to fight was called up. I volunteered anyway. In the same way my father volunteered for the First War. Even though he came back coughing his lungs up from mustard gas. Maybe that was why he felt he had to explain it to me. The only time he ever explained anything important. How you make yourself go over the top. He explained that to me – you have to bite the bullet.'

He chuckled. It was the first time I had ever heard Harry laugh.

'My God!' I was still trying to imagine it. I was trying to imagine somebody just my age going over the top of a trench into a hail of machine gun bullets. I just couldn't imagine it.

But Harry could see it clearly. There was a luminous glow in his eyes as he was talking. 'It was the closest we ever got to intimacy. A few minutes of advice. It was the most precious thing my father had to give to me.'

I was silent again for a little while, struggling to grasp what Harry was telling me.

'Something happened? Back then, during the war. Something that made the book special to you?'

'Oh, yes,' he said.

'You don't want to talk about it!'

He hesitated. And then he smiled. 'You're very clever, young Mylie O'Farrell from Sheffield. You see a man caught in the rain and you persuade him to let you borrow his hat. But now I am asking for my hat back.'

'What hat are you talking about, Harry?'

He was still smiling. 'The hat a man wears when another man has to do the talking. I've had enough of standing in the rain. I think it's your turn.'

I jumped off the edge of the bed and found myself standing in front of Harry's window, scratching my head.

'What do you want to know?'

'Why this doctor's daughter was attracted to the taxi-driver's nephew in the first place.'

'Shit!' I muttered, under my breath. I couldn't believe that he had remembered that.

I say, 'It's boring to talk about.'

I know that there are forsythias out there, through the window, little bonfires of yellow blossom, but I can't see them now in the dark. Instead, in my reflection, I am looking into the dark pools of my own eyes. I can't bring myself to look at him, to see if he is still smiling. I feel no desire whatsoever to talk about Tabi with Harry. But I don't think that I can refuse him, not after he has opened himself up in that way about himself.

'I'm sorry,' I hear him say. 'I can see that I've embarrassed you.'

Embarrassment isn't an adequate word for it. I just can't talk to him while facing him directly. It's easier for me if I look out at the grounds and the car-park through the window.

'Once she told me – Tabi told me – what it was about me that had interested her.' It's so difficult for me that I hesitate although I have no problem at all in remembering it clearly. I can hear every word, see every gesture. 'I couldn't believe that she had remembered something that had happened about two years earlier at the school.'

'Ah! You were in the same class, then?'

'We were in the same class for GCSE English literature. I remember having a blazing row with my teacher. His name was Mr Carr.'

I hear what could be a chuckle from the chair behind me. 'How old were you at the time?'

'I was sixteen years old.' I inhale in a sniff, then blow on to the glass, rubbing a hole in the condensation to look out through it. 'Anyway, this Mr Carr, he said I had an attitude problem that was not conducive to the proper study of English Literature.'

'And did you?'

'I don't know. Maybe I had at the time. Tabi, who was keeping her head down in the same class, was impressed by what she called my moral stand. Or at least that was what she told me later. She said she could never have stood up to a teacher that way.'

'Were you making a moral stand?'

'The truth of it is that I got mad with the teacher because of something he tried to make me say that would have been a lie. The whole class was asked to write an essay on a play by Willy Russell which is called *Blood Brothers*. In this play there are twin brothers, Mickey and Eddie. Eddie is given away to a rich family at the beginning, and grows up rich, while Mickey stays with his parents and grows up poor. The idea is to show how these two different social backgrounds give them very different philosophies of life. Eddie's philosophy, for example, is that we shouldn't take life too seriously. When Mickey tells Eddie that he is unhappy at being unemployed, Eddie reacts by saying, "Why is a job so important? If I couldn't get a job I'd just say, Sod it!, and draw the Dole, live like a Bohemian, tilt my hat to the world," and so on.'

'And you didn't go along with that?'

'There was more to it. I've just given you an example. I was being honest when I said to Mr Carr, "I really like the play in a lot of ways but I don't like it in other ways." For example I thought that the simple language Russell used to outline the plot worked pretty well as a contrast to the complex ideas that he was presenting. But I was disappointed with the plot. I thought the plot was a bit predictable. The problem was, I wasn't supposed to have opinions of my own. I wasn't allowed to say that I didn't actually agree with everything that Willy Russell was saying.

'Mr Carr said, "Somebody who is only doing GCSEs is not mature enough to say things like that." He told me he would downgrade me if I didn't rewrite my essay.'

There is the faint sound of Harry taking the twenty pack of Benson and Hedges from his pocket. The crackling as he tears off the cellophane. 'But you needed the good opinion of your teacher to pass your exam?'

I take a deep breath. 'I was so angry about it that I talked about it with my Uncle Tony when I got home.'

Tony was in his living room drinking a beer and watching a video of *The Godfather*. It was the first of the godfather films and the best. I think Tony must have watched that video about as often as Tabi watched *Truly, Madly, Deeply*. I remember the way he put his bottle down on the little side table and shook his head. I could see that he was trying to pouch out his cheeks like Marlon Brando when he said to me, 'Ah, sure – to hell with it, Mylie. That's what the teacher is telling you to do. If you went to one of them public schools, they'd tell you the working class is scum. So you can just do what the teacher tells you.'

I tell all this to Harry, minus the colourful language. And Harry, who must have gone to one of those public schools, is patient with me afterwards, during my contemplative silence. He makes no comment about Tony.

In the reflection in the window, I catch a movement of his hands, tapping the cigarette out of the packet. I hear the scratch of a match on the box. I smell the sulphur. I wait until I can smell the smoke of his first exhalation.

Tony could see I was really upset. What Tony did was, he went out into the kitchen to open the fridge and he came back with two beers, one of them for me. It was a bottle of Stella but I didn't want it.

'I had to sit down and I had to take away the criticisms and praise Russell like a genius for the excellent way he exposed the way your upbringing gives you your whole philosophy of life. I got a grade A for that heap of crap. But I didn't feel like studying much after that. To be honest with you, I stayed on to do my A-levels but I didn't do any real work after that because I thought that the curriculum had nothing much to teach me – or at least nothing that I felt it was worth my while to learn.'

Harry is smoking silently. Puffing away steadily, enjoying his first cigarette in over a month. I sense the wheels of his mind turning, at that same considered pace as he likes to read his book.

'So that was what she liked about you, this doctor's daughter? You were a bit of a rebel and she wasn't?'

'Maybe.'

'But you didn't go through with it? You gave in?'

'I needed the grades to pass my exam.'

'Your uncle was right. Your teacher was only doing what he thought best for you.'

'I suppose so.'

'Maybe you were wrong – in your criticism of the play?'

'How do you mean?'

'Your girl ... Tabi? She didn't agree with you. And the doctor's daughter subsequently went to university. The taxi-driver's nephew did not.'

I was shaking my head. Shaking it violently, surprising myself with the violence of my disagreement.

'So what is it? It aggrieves you now, the fact that you gave in on a matter of principle?'

'You didn't listen to me. Not really.' I couldn't hide my anger or my disappointment. 'Or if you did, you still don't know me very well, Harry. Not if you think I'm one for giving in.'

12

I am lying on my bed, still thinking about it. About the way Harry has of getting me wound up while also getting me to talk about myself.

What was he really asking me? I think I know. But I didn't tell Harry what he really wanted to hear. I'm not that stupid. There are things you can't easily talk about, even with somebody you like. Things that are so deeply personal you don't want to talk about them with anybody.

For example, I know that sooner or later I just have to face the truth about Tabi. I have been avoiding doing that all of the time I have lived in London. I know that makes me the biggest wimp who has ever lived but I can't help it, it's the way I feel about her. I'm not even sure I know how to describe to you the person that is Tabi.

I mean to say, how do you get round to really describing a whole person?

The answer is you can't. Not a real person. They are just too complicated. What we call a person, what we think we know well as a person, is like a bundle of things that we get to associate with them. That's what we recognise. We remember everything that happened, that maybe felt good about that person, that we felt were typical and we liked about them, but even all of that is a very small piece of the whole person. Do you remember that film, from quite a while back, called *Truly, Madly, Deeply*? Well, Tabi must have really liked it when she saw it on television because she recorded it on video, and then we watched it a lot. She must have made me watch it with her a hundred times.

It has Juliet Stevenson in it, playing a woman called Nina, who is grieving after the death of her husband Jamie, who is played by Alan Rickman. They have been so close, they have been head over heels in love with each other. So when Jamie dies, and Nina can't believe it, she just can't let go of what it was they had together. Tabi used to cry at the end every time, no matter how often she had watched it before, when Jamie tricks Nina into letting him go. He makes all these ghosts invade her house until she gets fed up with them. And then at the end Jamie's ghost watches her kiss her new man out there in the dark through the window.

Ah, Jesus!

The thing I am struggling to explain is difficult to put in words. It is so personal to her and to me that it hurts like hell even to begin to think about it.

It isn't just that I am being a pain or being secretive or anything, although I probably am, just a little. I could say it was indescribable, but that's the biggest copout, and the whole world would know it. It's the fact that I have to describe in words what I never really thought about in words. Things that we both felt. Embarrassing things.

So I'm just feeling my way towards it, doing the best I can. I am going to start by describing some of the things about her, some of the things that happened, and at least I can hope to get the simple things right.

Her full name is Tabitha Angela Mather. I think I might have already told you that she has long chestnut-brown hair, combed straight. Let me tell you that she is also very intelligent. She managed nine A's at GCSE and three A's at A-level. I know people who think you can get those grades if you work like hell, but you need intelligence too. What I am saying is that I don't think that somebody who wasn't very intelligent would get all those A's, no matter how hard they worked. There is another thing you would probably need to know about her, but you would have to know her well. That is the fact that she has this place inside her that she can go to. I mean a kind of spiritual place, or at least spiritual is the closest word I can think of to describe it.

That spiritual thing about a girl doesn't make it easier when you first get down to making love to her. It really doesn't make it easier for you at all.

There are all those books about love and films about it and all that. You know the sort of thing I mean, where this character gets his girl into bed for the first time and it's all good old rock'n'roll. Okay, so do you know what is the most painful confession I have to make? The painful thing is that with those girls, like Alison Morley, it was more like that. It really was closer to fun, up against a backstreet wall in the rain. I mean, girls like Alison took all the scariness out of it because they knew a lot more about it than I did. They have the same thing in mind that you have and they know exactly how to go about it. But Tabi hadn't done anything like that before. Tabi was a virgin.

That was something I discovered that night after I walked her home from the class party and we ended up climbing those stairs together.

I find myself asking her, 'Have you never done it with anyone before?'

And she is looking at me with these huge grey eyes, shaking her head and leaning against my shoulder.

'Bloody hell!'

So here we are, standing inside the door to her cold bedroom, surrounded by the black and whites of James Dean and the one huge colour poster from *Fantasia*, and she is actually trembling. The skin of her arms is covered in gooseflesh.

The bedroom is a regular dustbin, with clothes and stuff all over the place. For all of her intelligence Tabi is incredibly untidy. And I can smell those smells. There is nothing as powerful as smells in my memory of things. So I am smelling those smells reminiscent of my mother's bedroom - the smells of talcum powder and scent, and pot-pouri in the bowl on the dressing table. This only makes me more aware than ever of how nervous Tabi is feeling, of the struggle she is going through herself. I don't want to think about that at all. Now I wonder if it is Tabi I am smelling. I wonder if I can smell her more than the room, beyond the carelessness with perfume I noticed in the kitchen. I really believe I can smell the real woman. If I lick her skin, the skin I can see trembling against my shoulder, the skin of her face, her neck, her hands and wrists, her crotch – I know I will taste what I am smelling of her. It is her femaleness that is drawing me in through the smell of her skin.

Now I see the true reason for the tears a few minutes earlier. She isn't just excited, she is petrified. Her muscles are knotting up and jerking when I hold her, even as I am taking my first look around the room, surprised at the untidiness of it. Then turning back to look down into her tear-moistened eyes.

'It's okay. You don't have to do this, Tabi. It's no big deal.'

Shaking her head at this. The grey-blue eyes seem darker now, because the huge black caves of the pupils are swallowing up the irises.

Only later will I come to understand what is really happening here. That she has not travelled to Scotland with her father, although he must have pressed her very hard. That we will lie here, that we will literally sleep together, in the intimacy of her bedroom, that in an act of deliberate choosing, a seed has been sown in the deep instinctive female rhythm of things. That she, only seventeen years old, knows this better than I do as she puts on the Shola Ama CD, and she is sitting on the edge of the bed and starting to take off her clothes.

I have never seen a woman take off her clothes before. Certainly not purposefully like that. Not for my benefit.

I watch her in absolute amazement. That first glimpse of her determination. And the fact I can see the child in the woman, or maybe the woman in the child. I sit on the bed too and take off my top things and my skin is a ruck of gooseflesh. We are both shivering, waiting for the electric blow-heater to take the chill out of the air. At first I refuse to take off my jeans.

It will tell you something about Tabi when I explain that she still has two worn Teddy bears in her bed. I have to kick them out - slyly, so she won't even be aware of what I am doing - one by one as we are fooling around, before making love.

Tabi has a lissom feel to her body, that comes of having a swan neck and double jointedness. Her skin is white and downy although I have to admit she has a few small moles on her back. She doesn't often smile but when she does her whole face lights up into a surprised look, a look of wonder and giving. By nature she is every bit as secretive as Janus, but in a female kind of way. I suppose that what I am saying is that with Tabi there is a feeling, even on this first awkward occasion, that it has to be total, something she demands of me, as well as absolutely life-or-death secret.

It bewilders me that even in this first act of making love she is hungry for something she thinks she knows about me, maybe even desperate.

No girl has ever loved me before, so there is something wounding about it, something hurtable in its intensity. It is so cold we have to snuggle together under the bedspread. I have to guide her hand down there and then I shudder when her cold fingers close around it. But she has no idea what to do. She is too nervous even to explore. Her fingers are gripping too hard but I don't know how to tell her to ease up. I am too caught up in the clumsiness of it myself.

Shola Ama has got round to singing her cover version of the Randy Crawford song, 'You Might Need Somebody'.

There is such a look of concentration on Tabi's face. Not a word is spoken. It has gone beyond words and down to instinct. She never even asks me if I love her, so I don't need to lie to her. She doesn't tell me that she loves me. But that's okay – I know she loves me. One of the few things that men have an instinct for, I suppose.

But even for me there is something there already that goes beyond lust. A birth of something, quick and alive, like a hatchling bird's first spring into flight.

The only light is the bedside lamp and it throws shadows over our faces. She jerks or shudders every time I touch her. We laugh like idiots. Her shoulders, her belly, the small of her back. Her breasts, when I kiss the skin, feel as hard as wetsuit rubber, all grated with gooseflesh. And then, down below, I have begun to explore the sensitive valley within a valley, while she is playing this game they all play with you, of pushing my hand away at first, even though it is clearly for this that she has led me up those stairs in the first place. It isn't easy to enter her. We keep sliding up the bed and having to wriggle our bodies back down again, because she can't take the pain.

I look down at the top of her head, wondering. I ask her again, a whisper this time, 'Are you sure you want to do this, Tabi?'

Her answer is to bite the lobe of my ear.

Both her breasts are pressed against my ribs and her nails are like claws, gouging blood out of my shoulders.

And then, driven half mad by frustration, I push a brutal, desperate push and I feel it give way as she shrieks, and holds.

Tabi is still moaning afterwards, not just from pleasure but from the gradually lessening pain. And then, as I feel I should withdraw, she kisses me on the lips, kisses me hard, urging me onwards with her thighs. I can't believe it when she sighs. I have the wits to withdraw, hoping she is on the pill or something, because, of course, we are not using condoms.

Then she surprises me by asking, by whispering in my ear, by her sensitivity through all that has happened to my need. She takes over the reins then, finding the rhythm of it, until I sigh in my turn, my kiss devouring her kiss.

She slides out of bed to go to the bathroom. When she returns, she crouches over the CD to return it to that special track. She makes a point of choosing the track we will both remember, before curling around me, her hand below my neck, and whispers, 'Thank you.'

There is so much going on here. I know there is something going on that I don't understand as I lie there in Tabi's bed, smelling the smell of her, now mixed with the smell of toilet soap on her hands. We lie utterly still and silent for the few minutes it takes Shola Ama once more to sing, 'You Might Need Somebody'.

13

There's a stigma attached to being mentally ill. For example, when patients are admitted to a medical ward with an overdose and are told that they must be transferred to the Psychiatric Unit they are often very upset at first.

They will say, 'I'm not a mental case. There is nothing wrong with my mind.'

But once they have been admitted they will, for the most part, find the environment very friendly and restful. They get to like it so much they don't want to go home.

That was one of the things that surprised and impressed me when I first began to work here.

A lot of this has to do with the attitude of the staff, particularly the nurses. The nurses are great. They are fiercely protective towards the patients. They feel they get such a raw deal out in the community from people who are prejudiced against mental illness and that this even extends to when they come into the Unit.

One of the big issues at the moment, and it is especially the case on Gerries, is that the Unit gets served its meals last, often with lunches arriving as late as one o'clock. So the nurses on William Blake are organising a formal complaint to the hospital management about the catering department. Patients are asked to choose their menu for the day but they don't always get what they want. Nobody seems to be taking any notice of the fact that patients who are in hospital for months on end have special dietary requirements. Every day at least six of our patients end up with meals they haven't ordered because the food they wanted has already run out by the time it gets to us.

I was listening to Michael spelling this out on the phone – Michael, who is a nice guy most of the time but can be as bitchy as hell when has a mind to. He was laying down the law with the kitchen manager. 'Sometimes,' he shouted, 'it's no better than the leftover slops.'

Anyway, that was what was going on while I was enjoying my morning teabreak in the nurses' office, in the company of Alice.

Alice is the Jamaican nursing auxiliary who works all the time on Blake. She's fifty-seven years old. When I first came on to the Unit she was very helpful to me, doing some of my less pleasant jobs until I got used to it. She has a great sense of humour so we pull each other's legs a lot. You should hear her go when she is really laughing! She has a laugh you could bottle and sell for a million. Even the way she talks is musical. I could just sit back and drink iced beer and listen to Alice talking all day.

Suddenly there was a terrific commotion. It was going on at the bottom of the eight-bed dormitory, where two patients were screaming murder at each other.

'Hey, Mylie,' Alice said, with her dimples showing, 'you better get out dere an' shift some shit.'

She doesn't half love to wind me up. Piss I can stand, but shit makes me want to vomit.

I had just got out into the corridor when Michael confronted me with that artery jumping in his temple. He really has had some bad luck with his face, old Michael, which plays havoc with his love life. He has purple cheeks that are marbled by a million broken veins. It seems to me that Michael takes a regular hit in the heart when it comes to his friends, but still he carries on, doing his best for his patients. That's the kind of thing you should respect in people. I respect him quite a lot even though he gets on my nerves at times. Rumour has it that another of his boyfriends has deserted him and so today he was looking so browned off, what with organising the petition and everything, that I edged carefully past him so as not to irritate him further.

I was soon at the centre of the storm while Michael just stood there with his hands on his hips at the entrance to the bay, being sarcastic with Alice. I already knew from the voice who the troublemaker was.

Barney Silkes!

Barney should never have been admitted to an acute unit in the first place. He is seventy-eight years old and as venomous as a rattlesnake. He goes down the ward corridors attempting to kungfu-kick people. Only yesterday Harry had been moved out into the dormitory and that had made him fair game for Barney, who was hovering over Harry like a vulture, tugging at the shirt he was working on. You should see Barney's hands. He has really weird hands. He has fingers like claws, with yellow nails curling around the ends of them, and the nails on his two big toes are as thick and as ridged as sea shells. Harry had a tight hold of the other end of the shirt. There was a mad look in both their eyes. When I tried to take Barney's arm he lashed out at me with a come-on-and-take-me look in his eyes.

Let's face it, Barney is a lunatic. All the same, even though I knew that he was just a crazy old man, I wasn't too pleased with the way he was upsetting Harry.

But you just can't let the way you feel interfere with the job. That's something I have learnt from working on the Unit.

It was obvious what had been happening. Barney had been spying on Harry when he was cutting a hole out of the armpit of a new shirt.

Suddenly Barney began to screech with triumph. 'Look – look!' he gesticulated with his bony arm. 'Look at what the loonie's doin' to his shirt!'

The shirt business is a big thing with Harry. You wouldn't believe the concentration he puts into cutting those holes in the armpits. It's as if the pain that weighs him down is more than a physical pain. There isn't even a scar left over from that attack of the shingles. And I've noticed that if his attention is distracted, he stops moaning and leaning over. There is something very curious about Harry's pain – something secretive and personal. And there are aspects to his story that don't add up. You only have to think about the way he was on the floor fighting off six people when he came in and yet he hadn't managed to strangle Muriel in a whole evening.

I don't think I have got anywhere near to the heart of Harry's problem.

'Now who's a bad lad,' I muttered in Barney's ear. 'Time to go back to our little chair.'

'Leh go o' me arm!' Barney shrieked, staring back at me through his hair which had fallen in big silver peels over his eyes. I anticipated his trick of lashing out backwards with his foot and, when that didn't work, he tried to take a bite out of my hand with his false teeth just where I was taking a good grip on his arm. He'd eat you, old Barney, if he had the chance.

'How come yer aw'ways on 'is side, then?' Barney screeched, with his vowelly Cockney accent.

'The answer to that man's problem is a machine gun on a Sunday morning,' shouted Harry as I was shuffling Barney away, hissing like a snake, along the polished floor.

Of course quite a few of the patients had come to watch, clapping their hands and shouting encouragement. I got Barney into his chair and then he tuned up with a strangulated wheeze that would make you think he was dying. It would have been just fine if that idiot Harry hadn't picked his moment to start bawling. It was a tragic thing to see Harry crying his eyes out like that. I mean, he had a tear in his eye when he was admitted but he had never broken down and cried like that before. It was also the biggest mistake he could have made – all Barney needed to make a miracle recovery. He slipped out of my grasp and jumped up and down whooping, giving the football hooligan's rods towards Harry.

'Loonie! Loonie!' Barney crowed, as I shoved him back down once again in his chair. You could see where his dressing gown had drawn a circle around the floor in a snail-track of shiny piss.

'Isn't it marvellous!' Michael muttered from the corridor, before ambling off on his sandalled feet to get the drugs tray.

I screwed in the feeding tray across Barney' chair to secure him into it. Then, with that smooth way you only acquire from about a hundred years of practice, Michael sank a hypodermic of sedative into the thin leg sticking out under the tray.

Michael sloped off to the nurses' office, which is something he does when he's upset. I looked at my watch to confirm it was still only half past eight. Through the windows I could see that it was raining steadily. I wondered if I had time to sit in the office with Michael when I'd already had my break with Alice. You have to share Michael's endless cups of tea, which he takes to quieten his nerves. But still I was thinking about what Harry had told me - about his wife, Elizabeth and his son Teddy, living in Australia.

I waited a few minutes to give him time to calm down. Then I followed him into the office.

'He misses you, you know,' Michael said to me, sniffing a great sniff over his reading glasses. 'I think he's getting attached to your little visits.'

I watched Michael, who was sitting at the desk, reading Grumpy's notes on Harry. I guessed that he was puzzled by the same thing that was puzzling me. I know that Michael feels sympathetic towards Harry because nobody comes in to visit him. It struck me then that Michael must be much the same age as Teddy.

'What is it, this business with the shingles?' I asked him.

'I don't know,' he mused. 'People do get neuralgic pains for years after shingles.'

For a moment I studied the sign over Michael's desk, which read, 'THERE IS TOO MUCH WORRY GOING ON IN THE WORLD'.

I said, 'But Harry's pain seems to come and go. And what about those holes in his shirts!'

'It's probably a fixation. A compulsive ritual.' Michael began his own compulsive ritual, with the two mugs, the kettle on the floor and the cardboard box of Earl Grey tea bags.

I nodded because it made sense to me. I was interested in this notion of a compulsive ritual.

'Sometimes', Michael explained patiently, 'a physical symptom, such as a pain, is a referred symptom for a deeper, entirely psychological pain. It's called a hysterical conversion symptom.'

You could tell that Michael was gay just from the way he played around with making the tea. I watched this pantomime with amusement and I didn't say anything for what must have been a minute. I wanted to tell him about Harry's wife and son but I just wasn't able to break my word with Harry. And the idea that pain, real pain, could be psychological was very interesting to me. I was thinking about Harry and the argument between him and Muriel about the dog. To be honest with you, I was wondering if there was another reason, a much bigger and deeper reason, behind Harry's admission to the Unit than that argument about his dog, Nobby.

I had to endure a second mug of Earl Grey with Michael before I managed to break away and go back to talk with Harry. I knew he'd be feeling upset by the Barney business, and I had heard Michael tell one of the nurses to give him a sedative injection.

Then, when I went back to talk to him, I couldn't stand the fact that Harry was silently weeping. I could hardly believe that this man, who had talked to me in that very sensible voice only days ago, had broken down into this wreck once more. It seemed to me that the row with Barney had put him back down there into the bottom of his well. I was mad with Grumpy too, because I could see now that he had brought Harry out of the side ward too early.

'Young man,' he said, between his tears, 'there comes a time when you have to bite the bullet.'

I laughed, to make him feel it was funny. But he was deadly serious. He was sitting there slumped towards the window, looking out into the morning rain. Then he started complaining to me all over again about the fact that he had no money.

'What do you want money for, in here? People are looking after you. They're doing everything for you.'

'You need money', he said, not looking at me but still out of the window, 'if you want to go places.'

I told him that Patients' Accounts organised that. I had already told him about the safe on the ward, if he needed small change. If he needed more than pocket money for something, there was an accounts officer who would come to see him and sort it out for him. But he wasn't listening to me.

Then he started to ramble. I have never known Harry to make anything other than a kind of sense since the day he was admitted, but here he was describing how he had gone somewhere last night and he had found himself short of two pence. He said that he couldn't understand the fact he had money in quite a few banks and yet he was short of two pence. He said, 'I need a few pounds now to keep me going.' He talked about going out to the pub for a drink or to his local Sainsburys, to buy some biscuits for his dog.

'It's nice', he said, 'to be able to go out to the pub for a drink. Or to the railway station if you want to.'

I fished around in my pocket and found two pound coins and a fifty-pence piece – enough for a packet of cigarettes – to give to him. I gave him the money, although I knew he would promptly lose it. I had the lunches to organise but I didn't want to leave him like that. I was patient with him, explaining things that must have been explained a lot of times before. I told him he wouldn't be allowed to just walk out.

'Doctor Dury', I said, 'would have to sign for that.'

'Why?' he wanted to know.

'Because you're sick in your head, Harry.'

'But my head feels fine. I feel extremely well today.'

'You don't look so good.' I patted him on his left shoulder. I didn't know what to think. I mean, Harry's diagnosis is depression, but now he was sounding like he was developing Alzheimer's disease or something and not depression at all.

Then I remembered that Michael had sent one of the nurses to give Harry a sedative, so he was probably just confused by that on top of the antidepressant drugs. But still he got me worried, rambling away like that.

I said to him, 'Give it until tomorrow, Harry. Things will look different.'

He turned his eyes from the window and he was staring up at me out of his dejected position in the chair with a look of blankness in those blue eyes. Then the blankness invaded all of his face.

'I've looked into tomorrow. There's nothing there.'

'Hey!' I placed my hand on his left shoulder. I squeezed his shoulder.

'It's no good. I can't face any more tomorrows.' His eyes were slowly filling up with tears. It was happening in slow motion, the tears welling out of the blankness of his face.

I had to put my mouth up close to his ear so none of the other patients could hear me say it. I said, 'Now who's just giving in?'

Then he said, 'Son, help me to die.'

'Shut up, Harry!'

But he took no notice of me. He said it again, while I just stood there in absolute shock. He grabbed hold of my hand and he squeezed it.

He said, 'Son – promise me you'll help me to die.'

When it's two o'clock, I go home and I don't know what I am doing. People are staring at me on the 98 bus. I go straight to the cupboard where Janus keeps his Jack Daniels. I find a bottle he has barely touched, under one of his warning messages on yellow paper.

I lift the bottle out of the cupboard and I study the pint of amber liquid. I find myself reading some of the boring stuff you never bother to read on the label, about the fact that it was distilled at Lynchburg, Tennessee, using cave spring water. Then I unscrew the cap and take a swig from the neck of the bottle.

I carry it up to my room and lock the door and I lie down on my bed and hit the bottle. I've finished about a third of it in just a few minutes, but I don't find the place I am looking for. I play the CD, that is the greatest CD that was ever made, but not even Bob can do it for me any more.

About this time I hear Janus's shout, then the sound of his running footsteps on the stairs and his hammering on Rich's door. I take another swig out of the bottle, listening to them arguing on the landing, and then I wait for Janus to come hammering on my door.

I take no notice.

14

I was standing just inside the door to Michael's office. I would have preferred to hide my restlessness from him but there wouldn't have been any point in it. I said, 'What are we going to do about Harry?'

Yesterday I had failed to turn up for work, the first time ever, because I was half dead with a hangover from drinking a whole bottle of Jack Daniels.

Michael once told me I'd make a good mental nurse if I went for the training, so I knew that he liked me. He had been at this game a lot longer than I had. And now he was looking at me. He was reading my restlessness with the skill that an old farmer reads the coming weather.

'There are', he said, after some reflection, 'some very puzzling aspects to his case.'

'How do you mean, puzzling aspects?'

'Ask yourself this question,' he replied, still watching me speculatively over his reading glasses, 'is Harry basically a logical man?'

I hesitated, drawn deeper into the office. I slumped down into a chair.

'I'd say so.'

'So would I,' he said, ignoring the kettle on the floor. 'In fact, I suspect that Harry is more logical than most. Then we have to consider how he came into the Unit. We have to consider his behaviour on that particular day. He definitely didn't want to be admitted. He was fighting people to get out. There is a logical explanation behind his behaviour. So what we do is we look at his past life experience. That's where we are going to find the explanation.'

I nodded, taking this on board. This conversation was going to be the first piece of the jigsaw that would help me build up a plausible picture of the real Harry.

'Harry', I said, 'is a strong-minded man. But he's getting older. Things are going downhill in his life. For example, there's the diabetes and the cancer of his prostate gland. It can't have cheered him up to be told he was suffering from those two complaints. And the tablets he has to take every day are a reminder that he is physically sick. That he is a sick old man and growing older.'

'Right!' agreed Michael. 'Nobody likes to think of himself in this way.'

'I mean, you can see that. You can understand that. But there has to be more to it.'

I couldn't prove this, but I sensed it. I really did. There were aspects to Harry's case that I just didn't understand at all. I was thinking in particular about the strangling business with Muriel. And the fact he had let it slip that his real wife, Elizabeth, lived in Australia, with his son, Teddy. I mean, twenty-seven years is a hell of a long time for two people to live together and then break up.

We talked on, Michael and me, but we arrived at no enlightening conclusion. Except that I was sure now that there was something missing.

There is something wrong in all of this. There is something missing from the jigsaw. The trouble is that Harry is very secretive about his past - maybe too secretive. About his life in the army for example.

And then there is the book. Why do I get the feeling that something important revolves around the book?

So I have gone back to reading *Darkness at Noon*. I should have done so long ago, I know, because I am more convinced than ever that the book is vitally important to Harry. It really is a strange and powerful book. Almost immediately I come across this:

> *Ivanov had asked him to procure Veronal for him, and in a discussion which lasted the whole afternoon, had tried to prove that every man had a right to suicide.*

This is when Rubashov is brought in front of Ivanov for the first time. The first interrogation during his imprisonment. Or during this present imprisonment, because Rubashov has been in prison before. Old Rubashov has spent half of his life in prison. And there is something else, something I find particularly interesting. Rubashov is one of those people in the photograph of the delegates to the First Congress of the Party. Rubashov is one of the founders of the Russian Revolution.

You will have to excuse me while I laugh at this point, because this really kills me.

I am laughing because these men in the photograph are becoming extinct. They are fading out of the picture, one by one, as a result of what Koestler jokingly refers to as 'lead poisoning'. So in the end there will only be one face left: the face of No 1.

So now you know it is Rubashov's turn. This time it will be his face that will be rubbed out of the picture. That's the reason why he has been arrested. We have got to the place where Rubashov recognises his interrogator as his old friend Ivanov, the wounded officer who cried out for Rubashov to get Veronal for him when his leg had to be amputated in a war situation.

Veronal to help him die.

I knock on the door as usual.

It is late evening and dusk is falling. Harry is back in the side ward, in his chair facing the window. Michael has returned him there because he agrees with me that moving Harry into the general ward was a mistake. It was too early. I don't feel comfortable enough to sit on the edge of the bed and he doesn't feel comfortable enough to look at me directly.

I stand next to the window, looking out into the fading light. It is snowing in the grounds of the hospital so the ground is lighter than the blurred-out sky. After all the promise of early summer, spring has reverted to winter. It has been snowing for days in the middle of April. East Anglia is suffering the worst floods in a century and half the country is covered by snow. I hear a car door slam shut, like a muffled gunshot on the car park below. I listen for its engine starting up. At first I can't make out which car it is. I peer out through the chalklines of snow falling vertically on to the ground. Then the lights come on over in the corner. A small snow-covered mound shakes itself next to a snow-weighted clump of flowering currants. I watch it move slowly away, wipers gouging at the windscreen, tyres making snail tracks through the two inches of snow, heading towards the exit gate.

'Do you remember what you said to me?'

No reply. But there is that stillness again about Harry. There is one good thing however, in that I can tell that he isn't confused any more. So the confusion had to be caused by the sedative injection. But the distance is back in his eyes. The tension in the muscles under the puffy white face.

I remind him gently, 'What you asked me to do – it was a little bit silly, don't you think?'

'You come to see me. Asking questions. Always asking me questions.' Angry.

I watch the window winding down on the car. A hand comes out - an old hand (or so I imagine), the slightly shaky hand of an elderly woman. I watch the careful way her hand feeds the parking ticket into the key mechanism. The sudden jerk as the gate begins to lift. The painstaking way in which the car pulls out into the hospital road.

'It's my job to take care of you.'

He says, 'Poking. Prying.' Getting more and more angry.

'Would you prefer it if I stopped coming then?' I speak too quickly, too rashly, regretting it as soon as the words leave my mouth.

'But you don't like it when I ask you questions?'

I am silent.

'No?' He mocks. 'You don't want to talk about yourself?'

'You're not being fair, Harry.'

There is a half-smile on his face now. An unpleasant smile, devoid of humour. I look away, back to the window again. I hear another car door slam. I hear the ignition turn over. I see the lights come on.

'It's not so easy, is it, son, talking to some stranger about the things that really matter in your life?'

I cannot control the surge of anger in me, the resentment. The second car is slowing right down as it comes up to the ticket gate.

'Don't call me son, Harry. I'm not your son.'

I turn to catch that slow blink. The anger, the bitterness, already fading.

Am I being unfair to him?

Yes. My mind confirms it while my heart is still angry with him. He is silent for several seconds. A weight of lead is infusing the muscles of his face. It is dragging on the mask of his face so the skin falls and sags. It is an astonishing transformation, astonishing to watch the way it happens. You can't miss the leaden slowness as he takes a packet of cigarettes from the locker drawer. That same lead is in the muscles of his arms. I have the impression that he does it only to break the stillness of the silence. The glint of gold. He brings out the same gold-coloured packet of Benson and Hedges I gave him, only half consumed.

'Mylie, then,' he says.

He murmurs it softly, through this mask of pain. As if he has been thinking about my Irish name although it is only the second time in all of our conversations that he has spoken it.

I can smell that smell again. I didn't smell it when I came in. I am so shocked at my own angry over-reaction – so ashamed – I am suddenly flustered. Unable to decide what to say.

'You are not my doctor, Mylie.'

The words squeeze out with a terrible slowness, the message reluctant to cross the gap from his brain to his lips. They are heavy words, weighted down with lead.

'No, I'm not, Harry. But ... but I thought we were friends.'

I am overwhelmed by the act of witnessing his pain, that mental kind of pain that Grumpy talks about. I am smelling it, that mental pain. I am tasting it on my tongue. It is an anguish for me just to watch him take the cigarette out of the packet and lift it in that slow motion, that leaden motion, to his lips. I have to resist the urge to help him, to take the matches out of his lap and the cigarette out of his mouth. To light it for him with my own hands and lips. To rob him of the point he wishes to make.

I open the window a few inches, to rid the room of both tell-tale smells.

'You people here ...' he murmurs. 'You people ... in this madhouse ... asking me all these questions.' A pause, during which even the blink of his eyes is slow, the lead entering the tiny clockwork of his eyes. 'You poke – pry – into things. Every private corner and cupboard. You cut open people's minds.' A smoke. Then a blink. 'You expect us to just tell you everything.'

Of course he is right. That is what we do. That is what we do to people here.

I say, 'Maybe I should mind my own business.'

'Maybe you should.'

'Okay, Harry. So now you can get on with playing this stupid game of yours. Now you can just give up.'

It is incredible how, with that slow motion of anguish, the look of rage begins to gather. I watch the slow accumulation, the evolution, of rage in Harry's face. The slow-blinking aversion of his eyes. The fact that even this rejection of me can only be made to happen in that horrible leaden way. He is actually shouting at me, shouting in slow motion, shouting in words that take an eternity to form on his paralysed lips.

There are no words to Harry's shout. It is a nothing more than a mewling of pain, as if his despair has gone further than words could carry it. His face has become a torn and wounded landscape, a battlefield, over which his voice has become the howling of the wind.

15

Vera, the Occupational Therapist, is performing one of her tricks. I have seen her do this trick a hundred times but she is so good at it I just cannot help watching her closely. She breaks the lump of clay down into seven balls, one big one and six little ones. She rolls them around on the table surface, four little balls for each of the feet, the fifth for the nose. Then the sixth ball is split into two for the ears. It all takes her no more than a couple of minutes. If you haven't seen it before, it looks like magic.

'It's a pig!' exclaims Peter.

'Yeah,' I agree with him. 'It's a pig!'

I have been specialing the Reverend Peter Marlow, who has driven himself mad with his obsessive-compulsive disorder. It is a very interesting complaint, particularly in the way it shows up in Peter. If I weren't so confused about Harry, I'd be hitting the books on Peter's obsessive-compulsive disorder. But I can't focus my mind enough to do it.

One minute I feel so mad, the next minute I am feeling as guilty as hell. Guilty – I don't know what I am feeling guilty about. I have tried my best. I really have. All the same I just can't help worrying about the way I left Harry upset like that the other day.

So that's what I am worrying about, while Peter is admiring Vera's pig.

Vera is a stout, matronly kind of woman, with the most luxuriant red hair you have ever seen. We are sitting at the big central table in the Crafts Room. Behind us, through the wire mesh, you can hear the big pottery kiln roaring. I watch now as Vera hands Peter the balled-up lump of clay. I admire how she encourages him to make his own pig. I watch his hands start to mould the clay. Long bony hands, with huge brown freckles and veins that stand out like the roots of a tree. Still, it's a nice thing to see Peter smile, Peter glancing up at Vera now and then, at the love of her work showing in her big friendly face, all framed by that beautiful cataract of red hair.

First thing, after I arrived at 1.45 this afternoon, there was a message for me to go and see Michael in his office.

I sat there in a bit of a state, listening to Michael telling me to leave Harry alone. I couldn't believe he was saying this to me. Today of all days, when I was planning to go back and sort it out with Harry.

'Sorry,' he said. 'Dr Dury's orders.' He was tilting his head to one side and scratching his neck under the studs in one ear. 'Dr Dury is embarking on a course of deep psychoanalysis. You're not to see him for a while. Just for a while, Mylie. Leave it alone for a few days, okay?'

'Okay,' I said.

But it wasn't okay – something was wrong. I mean, something here stinks. Something here is being labelled 'Mylie's fault'.

In a way, of course, Michael is right. I just can't go about my work all the time thinking about Harry. There are other patients on the Unit and they need my help - what small help I have to give them. Mylie O'Farrell – the bum of the system.

So that is how I ended up here in the Crafts Room specialing Peter.

Although he looks like the picture of convention, with his soulful face and his short-trimmed curly grey hair, in fact the Reverend Peter has the most incredible imagination. This compulsive-obsessive disorder - you wouldn't believe the things it makes him do. Maggie was telling me about a condition of children called Gilles de la Tourette's disease. Peter's compulsions are very similar. There are none of the tics the kids get with Gilles de la Tourette, but it makes him curse and swear out loud. You can imagine the embarrassment if you are a minister of the Church of England and you can't help shouting out 'Piss!' in the middle of a service.

That was how his illness first showed up.

Peter has no control over this. It just happens out of the blue, as if he has lost control of his mouth to some goblin in his mind.

Knowing Peter, he would have managed somehow to cover things up for a while. You could just pretend to sneeze or to cough or something. You'd be surprised at how you could hide the occasional 'Shit!' and so on. But when whole sentences begin to come out, like in the middle of a service – or a sermon!

I'm not exaggerating. You can hear him these days from the other end of the corridor on William Blake, old Peter suddenly shouting out, 'Go and f*** off – go and have a f***ing good shit!'

Even I feel embarrassed. I'm afraid it would take a sneeze of genius to cover that up.

I don't know why Peter's illness makes him say these things. I wish I did. I wish I had the slightest inkling of what is going on in his mind. I mean, maybe it is some kind of twisted irony in a way, because he means the opposite of what he says. Or maybe it's just that there is a great pressure building up in there and it has to blow out in this peculiar way. All I know is that when you get to know Peter, you discover that he is a really nice man. You get to liking him a lot. If he were my minister, I'd just forgive him. I'd let him get away with his little outbursts. I would just listen to him swear and say, 'Amen' or 'God bless!' No offence or blasphemy intended. What I am saying is that a true Christian would want to succour him, but not, I regret to say, his congregation – or his bishop. They don't seem to be as understanding as they might be, in spite of the fact he has given his life to his church.

It's all those years, in Michael's opinion, that are responsible.

Michael is convinced that being a minister is the most stressful job there is. They are chucking ministers of all denominations on to the scrap-heap, according to Michael. They're dragging them down out of the pulpits and covering them up with blankets so they can hide them away in places like this. It's the long hours and the seven-day weeks and the fifty-two-week years. Even the ministers' wives, he tells me, all end up with these terrible consequences of stress.

I'd have been interested to talk to Peter about that but I don't think I should. Peter hasn't got a wife any more. Peter has been a widower for the last six years.

Back at The Palace, I tried to take my mind off things, playing cards with Rich and Janus and Rich's girlfriend, Angie, and her Eco-grungie friend, Pfion, who has recently come back from two years of studying the Native Americans. We played drinking games into the early hours of the morning. But I just couldn't get my own obsessions out of my head. I just couldn't help worrying about Harry. And that meant I kept losing rounds.

We were playing card games, like Chase the Ace, Touch Your Nose and Fuzzy Duck, where you rapidly switch direction around the table either clockwise or anticlockwise. The thing is you have to have your wits about you. I'm usually lightning-quick in following the change of direction, which is far from easy when the others are shouting to distract you. Last night I just couldn't concentrate enough, and so I kept on losing. And then I had to pay the penalty of chubbing my drink.

Chubbing is an utterly useless and meaningless sport where you suck out a vacuum in your half-full pint glass, so that it attaches firmly around your mouth. This makes your eyes pop out and your lips swell up, so your face resembles the fish. Then you hold your arms out wide, like a bird in flight, and, to the almighty chanting of 'Chub! Chub! Chub!', you glug the beer down through the vacuum.

And so by the end of the evening, thanks to Harry, I ended up bladdered out of my skull.

I don't even remember going to bed. All I can remember is waking up in a terrifying dream.

I found myself back in the graveyard where my father was being buried. It was raining, with a fierce mad glee, and all the while I had to sit there by my mother in the funeral car. I desperately needed to leave the car. I needed to see the wet soil falling on the coffin, because that was the only thing that would convince me Dad was really dead. But Mum was too upset to leave the car. And so I just couldn't bring myself to leave her.

That was when I woke up drenched in sweat and shivering.

I knew then, even as a kid of eight, the reason why Mum was so upset. She just couldn't accept the fact that Dad had died from something as stupid as a brain haemorrhage after taking part in an amateur boxing tournament. I didn't know why my father did it, not until much later, when my uncle Tony told me. It was the time when the east end of Sheffield looked as bombed out and ruined as it had been right after the war, because all the big steelworks were closing down. A great many people were out of work and my dad was one of them. Dad had been an amateur boxer back in Ireland, so he put his name down for the boxing tournament. I suppose that was why he refused to go down when he was taking a beating. He fought on because he was as angry as hell that he was out of work.

I realised in that moment in the funeral car that if we really do have souls, they are made up out of memories, of the terrible and the wonderful and even the ordinary memories of people that we care about. And when somebody you love dies, a piece of your soul is buried in the grave or burnt up in the oven with them. We are never entirely whole after that.

16

The very next day I was sitting with Maggie on Constable Ward. Maggie had dragged me into the kitchen. Maggie doesn't often drag me into kitchens. But our private discussion was interrupted when somebody started hammering at the door. I watched her open it and talk to Henry, who was determined he was going to come in.

Henry's full name is Henry Bright McClaren, and he's an out-of-work actor. He is twenty-nine years old and he is convinced that his life is a failure. Henry is a tall, lean man, with a springiness to his movements that makes you think of one of those plastic skeletons that is tied together with springs. I caught a glimpse of his shoulder-length straggly blond hair, balding at the front, and his thick ginger moustache.

Maggie said, resignedly, 'I know you're worried about going home tomorrow, Henry.'

Then he insisted on coming into the room. Maggie asked him to take a seat. He wouldn't take a seat. Not that it is unusual for a psychiatric patient to refuse to do what you ask him to do. What Henry will usually make a point of doing is sitting in your seat. And so here, today, Henry was making a theatrical point by staying on his feet.

Turning his face to the wall, he put his head in his hands, like, 'Woe is me!' He was just standing there with his head in his big red hands, bent right over with his neck muscles tensed. His face was also bright red –

his whole neck. Then he turned on the big performance. I don't know how he managed to do it, but he wept buckets.

'Please, Doctor Henessy – you've got to help me! I just can't stand it any more. The agony just grips me. You must give me some chemical relief.'

I could only admire the way Henry modulated his voice to an agonised whine.

'I need some comfort. Please – *please* – give me some chemical relief!'

Then he sprang into the chair he had previously rejected. He explained that his friend, Lawrence, had raped him psychologically and spiritually. Lawrence had abused and tortured him for years. Lawrence, I should add, is a small stout man of about forty, as docile as a rabbit. It seems that Lawrence, who works in publishing, is getting tired of Henry's sponging off him. 'I just can't go on any longer. Please – please, won't somebody help me!'

I was beginning to see why Henry was an out-of-work actor.

Maybe I was being a bit unfair on Henry, but my guts were really churning. When I am working lates, I usually get to bed at one or two in the morning and get up at about ten. But this morning, thanks to my dream, I was awake again at five-thirty and I couldn't get back to sleep again.

Henry began to strut about the room, all stoked up, and then he sat down and went through it all again, improvising here and there on the performance.

Maggie said, 'Are you anxious about going home tomorrow, Henry?'

He said, 'Home? I'm not going home to be tortured by that sadist. I'll kill myself first.'

He ran out of the room and we could hear his running footsteps along the corridor and down the staircase to the ground floor. I knew he was looking up at the window from between the rose beds.

First thing this morning, there was a 'round table discussion' about Lesley in the Quiet Room. Lesley has been getting better. You will remember Lesley, the DSH who swallowed the drawing pins and the light bulb. She has stopped doing dangerous things to herself and has come out of the Safe Room and returned to Constable Ward. So today the question was whether or not she might have reached the stage where Doctor Boyson would allow her out into the grounds under supervision. It would mark an important step on the road to her recovery.

Normally I would be very much involved in this. I'd have spent the evening before thinking about the meeting, so I might be able to follow the lines of discussion and maybe – only if somebody asked me to, of course – make some small contribution.

The trouble is, I have been getting so close to Harry and his problems that I have been neglecting Lesley. Of course I care about Lesley. My problem this morning was the fact that I was feeling pretty hung over again from drinking the night before and so I sat through the round table meeting and I never said a single word.

Maggie, of course, was at the meeting. I saw her looking at me every now and then. And as soon as the meeting ended and everybody went about their business on the wards – I, myself, sidling towards a quick mug of tea in the nurses' office – she grabbed me in the corridor, hauling me into the kitchen so we could discuss whatever was on her mind. It was clear that she wanted to talk to me privately, but Henry wouldn't give her the chance.

I watched her now, just after Henry had rushed out through the door, and while she insisted on pottering about, making me a mug of tea. Maggie doesn't make me mugs of tea.

'There's all this gloom about,' I said, conversationally. 'All these people talking about suicide.'

'Why? Who's been talking about it?' she quizzed me.

You have to watch yourself with Maggie. She's smart. Sometimes I think she can read my mind. I thought about telling her about Harry but it would have been breaking a confidence. Besides, she knew about him anyway. It was to prevent him doing harm to himself that Harry had been admitted to the Safe Room in the first place. I didn't want Grumpy to put him back into the Safe Room. I thought it would probably be the last straw.

So we talked for a while about this and that. It was all a little bit strained, this roundabout way of talking.

'Mylie', she said, suddenly turning serious on me, 'you know that I won't be around in a month's time.'

I could see the way she had to struggle with herself to say it. She couldn't even look me in the eye, so I knew that she was being as sincere as hell.

'Yeah. I know, Maggie,' I said.

It was her rotation. Maggie was only on the unit for a year on a rotation between different hospitals. I had known this all along, of course, but I had conveniently put it out of my mind. I wasn't too happy to be reminded of it, to tell you the absolute truth.

'It seems almost strange that I qualified as a doctor only two years ago, Mylie,' she said. 'It seems a lot longer than that. You wouldn't believe how nervous I felt. I felt incredibly nervous about everything. A few months before that I was just a student. Then right away I found myself thrown in at the cutting edge of medicine, dealing with life and death situations.

Honestly, I was petrified. I couldn't sleep at night because I didn't know if I had made the right decision or not. And if I made the wrong decision, somebody might die as a result. I was more nervous than a lot of my year, I suspect, and I drove my registrar mad always calling him out to check up on decisions I had made. What I am trying to say, Mylie, is that there is no easy way through it.'

I saw the way she paused then as she put her elbows on the table and made a cradle out of her hands so she could put her chin into it. Her head was curled down over her hands, like a little ball covered with dark fur. She is such a little person, when you take a close look at her, but she has real guts. That is what you can't believe about Maggie: that all that knowledge, all that determination, is bottled up in that dark little head.

'I know you care a lot about Harry,' she said to me. 'We all do, really. We all want to do what is best for him.' She sighed a great long sigh, turned up her face to look at me, then dropped it back down to hold it in her hands.

'What I am doing a very bad job of trying to say to you, Mylie, is that medicine isn't an exact science. We do things, we make decisions all the time, that are shades of grey. We make decisions that make a difference to people's lives. If you think too much about it, it drives you insane. So you have to learn the trick of detaching yourself in order to keep hold of yourself. Sometimes we make wrong decisions for all the right reasons. Most of the time, we hope, we make the right decisions. We all have to come to terms with that.' She stopped a moment and looked at me. 'Do you understand what I am trying to say, Mylie?'

'I'm not sure that I do,' I said.

Anyway, that was when Henry began banging on the door for the second time.

When Maggie opened the door, he threw a hat down on the kitchen floor. I picked it up. It was a plum-coloured wide-brimmed hat, all battered and flattened because Henry had been jumping up and down on it. I presumed that this must have been Lawrence's hat. He said, 'Show that to the doctor. Show her who she is talking to here. Tell her that she'll be responsible for what I'm going to do. Tell her!' He appealed to me, with a magnificent sweep of his arm, that went right over Maggie's head. 'Tell this ... this doctor ... that she'll have my blood on her hands tomorrow.'

We had quite a long talk after that, Maggie and me. She said she admired the fact that I had taken such a close interest in Harry. Michael must have been talking to her because she knew I had been visiting him regularly. Then she talked about Harry's illness. Harry was suffering from an unusually deep and chronic depressive illness. She talked about some of the chemical disturbances that went on in the brain when people were as depressed as that. All of this, as she explained patiently, made Harry's illness a particularly serious one.

I couldn't argue with that. 'I just want to help him, Maggie. I think it really stinks that he never has a single visitor.'

That was when, very purposefully, Maggie placed her hands down flat on the table surface and lifted her face again to look me straight in the eyes. She let the responsibility of her job show. I saw that look, the troubled honesty of that look, which she was allowing me to see. And I really appreciated this letting down of her defences. I think that in that one small action she gave me something I am really grateful for.

'We all want to help Harry, Mylie. We all do, everybody does. That's what we're here for.'

She opened her eyes wide at me for a moment, before dropping her face down again.

But she had said 'we' and so I knew now that Grumpy must have talked to her. I knew that he had talked to Maggie not just about Harry but also about me. Then I did something I should never have done, because it was a little bit unprofessional. I reached out and I put my hand over Maggie's where it lay curled up on the table surface. There was nothing sexual about it – or nothing I am going to admit to, because Maggie must be six years older than me. I did it because I wanted to communicate my respect for her. It touched me to feel how tiny her hand was. It felt little and cold. When I took my hand away she shivered, as if the contact between us had passed through her like an electric shock.

'I understand,' I murmured quietly.

'Oh Mylie – I hope you do!'

Then it was Maggie who reached out her hand to touch mine, shaking her head. 'I'll speak to Claudia. See if she'll visit his wife again.'

I hesitated, trying to take all of this into my bewildered brain.

'Thanks, Maggie.'

She said, 'Mylie – *Mylie!*' Shaking her head. 'I hope we all know what we're doing.'

'Hey – don't count me in, Maggie. I don't know what the hell I'm doing.' I grinned, nodding my head. Feeling overcome. Our eyes refusing to meet again.

'For goodness' sake, be careful from now on. What I've been telling you, about over-involvement ... Will you promise me that, Mylie?'

'Yeah!'

She hesitated, her face lifting, moved back to eye contact. 'I've been talking to Doctor Dury.'

I couldn't help still looking at her. Just looking at her face, searching her eyes.

'What's going on, Maggie?'

'Harry is going downhill.' She hesitated. Her eyes softening. 'We're in danger of losing him.'

'Oh Jesus!' I said.

'I'm afraid so. I've discussed it at length with Doctor Dury. We've decided to give him some ECT.'

My mind remained confused. I couldn't fully take it in. I didn't know what to think. I said, 'I'd like to go with him. Keep him company during the sessions.'

'What have we just been talking about?'

'But otherwise he has nobody, Maggie.'

'It's a nice thought. Really, it is. But Michael thinks it would be a bad idea.' She hesitated, still holding on to my eyes. 'And so do I.'

I was shaking my head from side to side.

'He needs somebody to reassure him. Somebody that actually cares about him. Jesus, Maggie - we're talking about ECT!'

'I'll talk to Doctor Dury. No promises!'

'Okay! But there's one more thing I would like to do for Harry. He's just been stuck in that side ward. Never going out. It's become like a prison to him. Honestly it has. Like a prison cell.'

She sighed. 'Well – what else are you suggesting?'

'Just let me take him out into the grounds. In between sessions. So there isn't just that empty side ward for him to come round to every time.'

'I'll see what I can do, but I'm making no promises.'

'Thanks, Maggie,' I said.

17

I had just brought Harry down to the Treatment Suite for his first course of ECT therapy. Now I was reassuring him as I wheeled him into the waiting room, with its cerulean walls and its carpet the colour of a hay-field. 'It's not at all like you might imagine,' I murmured, comfortingly. Harry was perfectly able to walk, but Maggie thought the wheelchair prudent.

'Honestly, Harry! There's no pain or discomfort whatsoever. You just wait and see. Everything is going to work out fine.'

The anaesthetist hadn't arrived yet and I helped him to his feet so that he could walk straight into the treatment room. He nodded tiredly to me and then lay down on the paper-covered couch. Next to the couch we keep the treatment trolley covered up by a length of green couch paper so that the sight of the equipment won't frighten the patients.

That was when the anaesthetist arrived, in perfect time to introduce herself. Doctor Thompson asked Harry if he understood what we were about to do, talking through the usual explanations. Harry didn't seem to care. He just nodded away, sighing now and then, so I could tell that he wasn't really listening.

Doctor Thompson is a bit of a fusspot, always insisting on getting everything perfect. She started off by clipping a connection shaped like a clothes peg over Harry finger. This is a pulse oximeter, which measures the heartbeat and the oxygen level in the blood.

Sometimes the pulse goes up like a rocket. Then she put a tiny blue needle, which they get off the kids' ward, into the back of Harry's hand.

'Hold on to his arm for me, will you?' she said to me.

I clapped Harry lightly on his good shoulder before squeezing his arm just below the elbow, just tight enough so that Dr Thompson wouldn't need to use a tourniquet to make the vein stand up. The muscles of his arm were as tense as hawsers. I felt so nervous, to tell you the truth, that mine were probably just the same. Next she filled up Harry's lungs with oxygen, because he would stop breathing during the fit. Then she gave him the injection, very slowly. The injection was a fast-acting anaesthetic. She changed syringes to give him a second shot to relax the muscles, so that Harry wouldn't injure himself with muscle spasms.

Although Harry still didn't appear to be listening, Doctor Thompson talked to him all the time she was waiting for the effects of her 'little injections'.

Then it was time to ask the patient to count back from ten but Harry wasn't counting.

As soon as he went off to sleep, I brushed his eyes closed, trying to hide the fact my fingers were shaky. Then I uncovered the trolley. You have to work fast because the anaesthetic only lasts for a few minutes. I hauled it up next to Harry's head and watched Maggie go to work.

The electric shock machine is like a box with two dials on the front and a green flashing light. One dial has three settings: OFF, TEST and ECT. The other dial has settings in millicoulombs. There's a little green light that flashes. The current is applied through two paddles with black handles, which have terminals about an inch and a half in diameter that are covered with contact sponges. They could be giant earphones, with those sponges on the end. These are kept in a pink conducting liquid that looks just like the stuff you wash your mouth out with in the dentist's surgery. It's very important to get a good connection with the patient's head. If you don't get a good connection the current will spark all over the place.

The black trigger buttons are about halfway down the handles, so that they go between your fingers when you grip them. I watched how carefully Maggie picked out her two positions, holding the paddles on either side of Harry's head. *Good old* Maggie, I thought, even though I couldn't help but notice how difficult it was for her, with her tiny hands, attempting to press the electrodes on hard.

You should have seen how determined she was with the paddles, all the while keeping her elbows close to her sides.

Her arms were juddering from trying to apply enough pressure so it was a relief to me when she triggered the black buttons. But she couldn't let go immediately. She still had to keep the electrodes pressed tight into Harry's head until a sound appeared, like a medium pitched whine, which tells you that the electricity is flowing. I could see when the fit was starting because Harry began to jerk. Then Maggie had to keep holding on tight until the sound stopped, which needed another five or six seconds. Maggie took particular care to make sure that Harry received the maximum charge. All new patients are supposed to get 200 millicoulombs.

When I saw my first ECT case, I was expecting the patients to jerk and jump all over the place. But they don't throw an almighty fit, as you might expect with somebody who didn't have the muscle relaxant.

It's all very carefully controlled. As soon as the sound stops you start timing the fit.

I helped Maggie to time the fit, watching until the big toe of Harry's right foot stopped twitching. It was spot on thirty seconds. 'Okay,' she said. 'You can take the paddles.' I accepted them out of her hands while she was reading off the machine, so she could mark down how many millicoulombs she had delivered.

Often when I watch SHO's do ECT, they only manage to deliver about 165. Most of them are women and they are just not strong enough. Today Maggie managed 199 and I was really proud of her.

18

'You see!' I said to Harry. 'Things are not looking so bad, really.'

But he, of course, was refusing to answer, just grunting now and then in the wheelchair when it jerked as it went over a bump. Harry was annoyed with me because I had had to be a little bit forceful earlier, making him put his pin-stripe jacket on over his shirt. I had to park the wheelchair outside the door to his room, waiting in a kind of mute conspiracy, with its brake on.

Of course Harry was perfectly able to walk, but this was his first time out in three weeks. And he needed the jacket. It was still just the last week in April, although the sun had banished every trace of the recent wintry snap.

We were going down in the lift to the ground floor. I waved to Anna as we arrived in Reception. Then we were through the twin glass doors into the vestibule, with its map on the wall and the drinks dispenser, and through the second doors. We were rolling down the corridor that leads to the side entrance and already we could see the flowerbeds.

And then I was chuckling even as I was struggling through the door. I was kicking it back with my heel to start it on its closing arc, and I couldn't help exclaiming, 'Look at that sky, Harry. Just look up there at that sunny blue sky.'

Before us the rose beds were puffed up with colour. Four crescents to either side of the big circular one, four quarter moons.

'If you ask me, it's going to rain.'

Ah, well! Let him grumble. Harry had been grumbling all the time I was getting him ready. Grumbling to Michael as I was wheeling him past the nurses' station because he didn't want to stay in the wheelchair. As if he were able to walk outside all by himself. He hadn't wanted to wear the plaid jacket because it didn't belong to him. He hadn't wanted to go out in that jacket. Not one word of thanks that Grumpy had given him the pass to go out.

I didn't mind Harry grumbling. It was a major improvement on the last time I had seen him. I was aware of where he had been yesterday. The second of six bolts of lightning through his brain. The countdown on his big toes twitching.

I was making a little detour around the rose garden with its great circle of the central bed, between it and the crescent moons. These were a blaze of late-flowering creamy daffodils and the eye-dazzling red and yellow of tulips. Harry made no attempt to touch the roses. He didn't lift his head so he could look up at the sky.

I began to tell him a tortuous joke about the old time comedian Tommy Cooper, who had a clown's face without needing a mask. Tommy died on stage with his feet sticking out through the hastily pulled curtains. Everybody thought it was another of his jokes. Tommy is stopped by Saint Peter at the Pearly Gates. Saint Peter will not let him through until he gets one joke right. So Tommy pulls out the deck of cards and asks Saint Peter to pick one. Tommy goes through the entire deck, getting every card wrong. That, of course, is the point of it all. Tommy Cooper's jokes always went wrong. Saint Peter says, 'Sorry', but Tommy asks for a second chance. Because his antics have so amused him, Saint Peter gives him a second chance. This time Tommy calls every card the three of hearts.

Harry listened but he did not laugh.

'Hey, come on. Things are looking up. Even you have to admit that.'

Another groan, because I had hit the hard edging of a flower bed with one of the wheels. 'Thank you!' he exclaimed. We were back to the old clipped officer's bark. His voice was pained, rasping, as I wheeled about, heading for the north end path. 'Do you know who you remind me of?'

'Who's that?'

'Oh, just somebody.' Falling back into grunting again, the bald head sunk down on his shoulders. I was looking down onto his pate of freckles.

'Come on then – who do I remind you of?'

'Montgomery – the commanding officer. Old Monty! Before we went on board the ship.'

'What ship are we talking about, Harry?'

We were about halfway along the north wall of the Unit. A hilly green lawn extended between us and the circular road that led to the main car park.

'The ship for the D-day landings. I suppose you might have heard of the D-day landings?'

'What landings were they?'

'Go to hell!'

'Oh, go on then! Let's hear about the D-day landings.'

'The Green Howards,' he continued, menacing me to seriousness, 'had been to hell and back, long before Operation Overlord. The 50th Division. In North Africa and Italy.'

'Italy, huh?' I was thinking about my Irish grandfather.

'Four battalions sailed out of Liverpool. They fought at Dunkirk, were among the last formations to leave. They fought for Montgomery in North Africa, El Alamein. Then Sicily. Again for Montgomery. Always for old Monty.'

He paused now. I could see that he was deeply involved, deeply emotional.

'He wrote Major General S.C. Kirkman a letter, Monty did, praising the way the 50th Division had fought. But only two out of the four battalions came home.'

I had to take a pause myself, to decide on a direction. I continued walking, pushing him along in the wheelchair, holding on to my silence.

'The survivors,' he groaned, 'the veterans, they were worn out. The new battalions had to be made up, fifty-fifty, with raw recruits. We were two of them. Myself and my friend, Froggy Pritchard.'

Another groan as we passed by the far corner, into the flatter, more open garden area, where there were rowan trees around the curves of the path, with delicate buds about to open. 'We thought we were going to escape the first assault in Normandy. But Monty decided he needed the experienced troops so he came along to talk to us.'

Another pause. He was gasping a little. He appeared to be gasping for breath.

His voice was suddenly low-pitched. 'We were all gathered together in a clearing in the New Forest, near Southampton. We had been treated to demonstrations of new weapons. A tank that poured out a sheet of flame into a pillbox.' Hesitating now, imagining, or so I thought, there were German soldiers in that pillbox. 'There was another tank, an amphibian, that could come up out of the sea and roll on to the beaches. One with chains, that would cut through minefields.'

Harry's voice was croaking, struggling. 'He told us to take off our steel hats. Everybody. There must have been a thousand of us, standing in lines. Even the top brass. He turned to the senior officers and he told them to take off their hats. Even a general from HQ, who was standing beside the staff car.'

Another bump, as we crossed over the hump of a drainage gutter, Harry muttering oaths. To our left, over a fence, was the vegetable garden with its greenhouses, where some of the patients were enjoying their occupational therapy. Another bump and another groan from Harry. It was hard to focus on my prime directive against the emotional blackmail of this grunting and groaning.

'Are you listening to me? Do you want to hear this or not?'

'Yeah. I want to know why you had to take off your hats.' I had to stop pushing him, otherwise he wouldn't explain.

His voice was soft. All of a sudden it was reverential.

'He walked down the rows of men. Each man he looked direct in the eye. He came to me. You weren't supposed to look back at him. You weren't supposed to look him in the eyes. But I did. He had blue eyes the colour of tempered steel. They looked hard into me for what seemed to be a long time. He didn't speak at all. Perhaps I wasn't worth speaking to. Then he went back to the front, climbed up on top of the tank with the flails and he told us all to gather round. He said, "Now I have seen each and every one of you. I will remember your faces the next time we meet."'

I had to start pushing Harry again to cover up the fact I had started to laugh. I just couldn't help it.

'Did he really say that, old Monty?'

I was distracting him as we bumped over another edge to climb on to a path.

'He seemed so full of confidence. He said to us, "We are going to knock Gerry for six."'

'Get away!'

'That was exactly what he said. His exact words. "We are going to knock Gerry for six."'

'I believe you, Harry.' My words were bubbling out through my laughter. 'You've got to hand it to him - it was a smart move.'

'He was so full of confidence. It was all so simple to him.'

'Yeah,' I said. I was struggling to figure out how to deal with this. To Harry this was deadly serious. I could sense his rising desperation.

'It was a trick. A trick of words.'

Harry didn't mean a trick of words. What he meant was a play of ideas. The idea that every one of those men was important to Montgomery. But you had to admire the way he left every soldier believing that he knew him personally, expected of him personally.

'I really am pleased, Harry, that you're comparing my tricks with those of Montgomery.'

'Don't flatter yourself.'

'But you have to admire the man. He was good at his job.'

'He was brilliant. The men loved him. They would go anywhere for him. Later on, I discovered that he was a very difficult man to work alongside. There were those who said he was conceited – conceited and arrogant.'

'Maybe he needed to be.'

'Perhaps he did.'

I was divided in my mind between keeping away from the painful subject of war and having to humour Harry. From the kitchen conversation with Maggie, I was aware that Grumpy knew all about Muriel and Harry's wife, Elizabeth, and his son, Teddy, who lived in Australia. Of course Claudia must have found this out when she went to visit Muriel.

I paused to give him another small break. 'How are you feeling?'

His face was momentarily radiant, lost in his war memories. In his meeting face-to-face with Monty. He had withdrawn from me again; he was refusing to speak to me.

Suddenly the sun was shining. A beautiful promise-of-May sun. It felt as if hope had broken through the clouds. As if this were the strong pure light of hope shining directly on to my face.

'Did you ever meet him again - old Monty?'

'He never stood up in front of us like that again. But I saw him in the distance, a year later. At the victory parade.'

We had arrived at the straight bit now, the stretch that runs along the side of the main drive. I couldn't help thinking about the lovely Anna – the way she had waved to us in Reception. There was a bit of tension developing around Anna, which I didn't want to think about at that moment.

'That trickster!' muttered Harry suddenly. 'Playing word games like that.' Harry muttered this with a growl that was half grumbling and half exultant.

'Nobody is ever perfect,' I said. Laughing too. Laughing with him, because nothing was to be allowed to upset Harry on this glorious day. No mention of Muriel. No mention of his wife and son. And this discussion of the war was not taking place.

Nobody knew anything about the book. Not Michael and not even Grumpy. Nobody except me. And I knew that the war was linked to the book. The book and an officer in the Green Howards, whose first name had the initial 'R' and whose surname was Giles.

Harry was suddenly groaning. He was almost crying aloud.

'What's up? What's the matter?' I had to park the wheelchair against the grass verge under the shade of a small sycamore. I was hunching down on one knee, looking with concern into Harry's pain-racked face. He emitted a wet, extremely foul-smelling fart.

'That poofter with the rings in his ears. Told them to give me three Dulcolax last night. I thought they weren't working.'

'Oh, shit!'

That's one of the things about Michael. He's a bit of a bowel fetishist. Now I had the explanation for all of the groaning and grunting – Harry had the gripes. I was desperately looking around me, wondering what to do.

To our right it was no good at all. Just the four-storey gable end of the main hospital buildings. Across the drive were some old buildings - a jumble of blackened stone with blue slate roofs. The groundsmen's corner. I was hurrying. I was just about running, to be honest with you, pushing the groaning Harry ahead of me in the wheelchair.

My eyes were riveted to this small building on one side, like a lean-to, built out of red brick. It had a green-painted door, with a gap at the top and bottom, and a trapezium cut through the planks at about eye level.

'Hold on, Harry!'

We just about got there. I slammed the brakes on. I had to hope the thing was what I thought it was and that it was unoccupied. I shoved him in, glimpsed the old white porcelain pedestal, the verdigris-encrusted chain hanging from the cistern about eight feet above the floor. No paper. I barely had time to register the fact that there was no paper as I shoved Harry forwards, leaving him staggering against the wall with his trousers coming down.

Then I was sitting in the wheelchair myself, just about gasping, when a man aged about fifty-five, with a thick head of wiry grey curls, came out of the building up the path to ask me what the hell was going on. Jumping up out of the chair, I could only apologise, explaining that Harry was a patient, caught short while I was walking him around the grounds. His grounds, which I now effusively praised, since he was obviously the head gardener.

He said nothing, looking me up and down. He could hardly miss the fact that I had no uniform. That fact was now registering that we were from the psychiatric unit. Perhaps he was nervous of this lunatic in there, invading the privacy of his territory.

I hardly needed to explain, because there was such an explosion of sound and stinks coming out of the bog, through every gap and crevice in the door. Suddenly I was grinning. Suddenly I was laughing so much there were tears in my eyes.

'If we could borrow some paper?' I gasped.

He was a decent sort in spite of the gruff voice, and he went back into the building and brought out a half-used pink roll, its edges laced with garden dirt. I had to squeeze it into an oval to pop it through the reeking trapezium in the door. Then I saw the coil of smoke coming out through that same space, which told me Harry was celebrating with a cigarette.

'Thanks, mate!' I said to the grey-haired man. I was still shaking my head, still grinning. 'If you wouldn't mind, maybe we should hang around for a few minutes – to be on the safe side.'

'Just tell him to leave the paper there, what's left of it,' he said.

I started laughing again. I just couldn't help it. His face was without a crinkle of a smile, which to me was frankly unbelievable. He nodded towards a worn old path that wound towards the back of the complex of buildings.

'Take him up there,' he said, 'if he needs a rest. It's out of the way. Stay as long as you need to.'

The first thing that Harry exclaimed, as I wheeled him around the corner, was 'Jacaranda!'

I was equally astonished, to tell you the truth. Astonished at the discovery we made here, in this forgotten corner of the hospital grounds.

It was a wild place, hidden behind functional buildings and in the shadows of trees; a place that no longer belonged in the modern hospital, a relic of what must have been a cottage and its garden, swallowed up when the workhouse that would later evolve into the hospital had devoured everything within half a square mile of its founding. A place that had somehow held on to the broken paving stones in a narrow path, with a little vegetable garden to one side of it in which two flowering cherries and an old pear tree had survived. My eyes discovered a dry-stone wall, a small surviving section no more than eight feet long, kept together as a seat by generations of groundsmen.

I could read the empathic reaction in the eyes of Harry as we left the wheelchair to one side, to wander into the narrow enclosure, with its weed-strewn ground amongst blossoming trees. We sat down, side by side, on the two foot wide dry-stone wall, which was covered with time-worn coping stones, each stone as broad and long as a flagstone and fully four inches thick.

I could see from the ebbing of tension from his posture, as he took a cigarette from the packet, that he welcomed it as much as I did.

'Which of us is wearing the hat, Harry?' I smiled, then grinned. I was shaking my head in disbelief.

'I think', said he, 'that hats are not required here.'

19

Harry is sitting on the dry-stone wall. His jacket is nearby, folded up, where I placed it on the seat of the wheelchair. He is watching a movement in the wilderness of grass, under the shadow of the pear tree. A white cat, its coat as dull as flour, has been interrupted in its stalking of a tortoiseshell butterfly. The cat turns, as if it senses our eyes upon it. Its yellow eyes, the colour of butter, move from face to face, from eye to eye, its half pliant, half devouring nature evident in the stare. It is feral, as wild as the weeds that proliferate here. Even the coping stones that cover the two foot thick dry-stone wall are old, maybe two hundred years old or more, and covered with the flat petals of lichens the colours of mustard and lime-green and milky silver.

Harry has had to pay one more visit to the lavatory before he can feel comfortable. I have waited for him here, sitting on the wall, amazed at the discovery of this place. I can confirm that it has definitely been a garden. A cottage garden. I wonder in a little more detail about the grey-haired gardener and his assistants. Why they have permitted this tiny corner of the grounds to remain untended? Perhaps because it is not visible. They don't need to bother about this place, which is out of sight. And yet here, by the low wide wall, feet have trailed from people sitting. I can see the evidence of this. The bare earth, compressed like brown pottery clay, ready for firing. Sitting, relaxing, smoking – to judge from the ash of pipes and butt ends of cigarettes – and perhaps contemplating this liberation from their daily routines of tending and weeding in the grounds of the hospital.

'It reminds me of my grandfather,' I say to the returning Harry. 'His allotment, which was about three miles away from where he lived. He used to travel to it on a big black bicycle. He carried me on the bar when I went to stay with him, when I was eight years old.'

I have been reminded of this, this other curious thing. That my grandfather, who was a born gardener, also allowed the part of the allotment where he sat and smoked his pipe to grow wild.

'You were close to your grandfather?'

I recall what I can about him. His name, Paddy, short for Patrick. The smell of his pipe tobacco. He was a stringy, grey-haired man, with large, bony hands. Hands that remind me of my own hands. A certain distance about him. The soft, strong Irish accent.

'I was a disappointment to him.'

'I find that hard to believe.'

I look away from him in silence, a silence neither of us wants to break for a while

'Tell me a little more about yourself. About your family.'

'There isn't much to tell, not really.'

His question bothers me. I don't like to talk about myself. I know now that this is a thing that Harry and I have in common. Like the gardeners, we keep our intimate places out of the way, as invisible as possible.

'You were born and you grew up in Sheffield?'

'Yeah.' I hesitate, a few moments of reflection. 'In the same house. On the Abbeydale Road.'

'Tell me something about Sheffield, then.'

'What is it you want to know, Harry? Is this some kind of interrogation?'

'No. I'd just like to know more about you.'

'Sheffield?' I say hesitantly, reluctantly. 'I'll tell you the commonest misconception people have about Sheffield. They think of it as a filthy place, just another grimy industrial city. But it is also a city of trees. Just about every street in Sheffield has trees growing in it – even the Abbeydale Road.'

'You seem very proud of it.'

'I'm not saying it's perfect. It was the last big city in Europe to get an airport.'

The tension erects a silence between us. I study the pear tree. Wondering how old it really is. Wondering, can you tell its age from the fissures in its bark?

'Tell me about your grandfather – the Irish soldier.'

I sigh then, because I knew this was coming, just as I know that Harry will not let up. 'I can't tell you anything about the soldiering part of him. He never talked about it.'

I just cannot believe the way the tree leans over like that. I hunch down to examine it. The fissured hole near to where the knotted trunk comes out of the ground, bent and crippled here where there should be a main trunk. A side branch has taken over the major burden. I can make out the huge scar where the original trunk once stood, broken off in some storm a century or more ago. How has it regrown like that? How has the stressed wood in the side branch survived all that weight hanging away at an angle like that? Withstood it for a hundred years?

'You said he was a gardener.'

'It seemed like magic to me. My father was useless in the garden. We had a garden behind the house but it was covered in pieces of old motor bike. I remember once, after I got back from visiting my grandad, I went out to a shop and bought some seeds. I thought they were cabbage seeds, because of the picture on the packet. In fact it said kale on the packet, but I had never even heard of kale. I thought it was another word for cabbage. So I cleared an area and I planted the kale.'

'Did it grow?'

I laugh - a short, triumphant laugh. 'It grew all right.'

I can remember the little sprouts coming up. I'd be up at cockcrow every morning and out to have a look at them. Watering them from a milk bottle. Watching them grow.

'Perhaps you should have become a gardener.'

'Maybe I should.'

There is a prickle of anxiety deep within me, which comes from talking about myself and my family. All the same it is so relaxing. I have never spoken to anybody in this way about my childhood before. Harry is sitting on the low wall, smoking. I am standing in the dappled shade, under the foliage of the leaning pear tree, watching him for a moment or two. Harry is not looking at me directly. I study the arc of his arm as he brings the cigarette to his mouth. That odd way he has of holding it, so the glowing ember is cocooned, like the primal spark of life, within the cradle of his fingers. Like my grandfather. The noise he makes inhaling, not giving a damn what harm it is causing in the depths of his lungs, as if he needs the damage of the smoke in the depths of his lungs to reassure him that he has risen above his fear of death.

'There was a wild cat, too. Just one cat. I called it the Yeti, because it had thick fur that stuck up, like an unshaven hairy face.'

Harry chuckles. 'I see,' he nods, 'that we have a whole family of them.'

He's right. There is more than one feral cat. While we have been talking, at least three more have appeared. Three are dull white, like the first. Two of these fairly young, judging from their size and their inquisitive behaviour. And one old cat, presumably the mother, banded in complex greys and brown. I think it is what people call a tabby cat. It must live here with its brood. The wild garden is their hunting ground.

'I remember', I am fighting nettles with my boots, clearing a safe patch under the old pear tree, 'he grew tomatoes in a greenhouse.' The pear tree is fascinating me again. It really is amazing. The main trunk, what is now the main trunk, only rises about two and a half feet from the ground before it becomes almost horizontal. Then it runs for about three or four feet before rising vertically, its main branches folding back upon itself, so the main mass, the centre of gravity, comes back over the point where it emerges from the ground. Its bark is scored like an alligator's skin, with crevices that penetrate deeper. It looks incredibly old. I test its strength, the horizontal section, to make sure it will bear my weight. It is just detectably springy, resonating like a taut spring to the force of my boot. Reassuringly so. I sit down, cautiously still, on the slightly uncomfortable surface of its fissured bark, testing the springiness once more. I try to think back to that first time in Tramore, when I was so upset after the death of my father. I begin to swing one leg over the flattened nettles and big heads of wild grasses. 'I never saw tomatoes growing before. I'm not sure how I thought tomatoes came into being. I can remember –' my hand is waving in the air - 'I can remember this sense of wonder. It was as if I were seeing a miracle. My grandad saw it in my face, I think, because he reached up and picked a couple for me.'

I have forgotten that it ever happened until this moment. Now I am there again. I feel his presence close to me. The smell of his pipe. I remember the twist of his wrinkled neck. His contemplative silences. The tomatoes, just approaching ripeness, in my hands. I couldn't bring myself to bite into them.

'Go on,' Harry is smiling.

From the look on his face he is imagining it in his mind. He is smoking another cigarette. I notice the different way he holds the newly lit cigarette, the normal way, with the burning tip exposed beyond the knuckles, the smoke trailing faintly in the bright hot sunlight.

'He handed them to me – the tomatoes – and I remember looking down at them. The greeny redness. The feel of them, the roundness. I ran out of the greenhouse, still looking at them. I didn't want to eat them.

'When I bit into them, it was with the same reverence I had, as a child, for Holy Communion. As if they were the creation of a god. They tasted bitter. I almost spat the first taste out. But I could see him watching me, so I didn't let him see me spit it out. The bitterness no longer mattered to me. I ran and jumped around, between the growing onions and the flowers of the peas, the cabbages and lettuces, with the greenish-red innards of the tomatoes running down my chin.'

'He must have liked that. He must have enjoyed taking you on to his allotment.'

'Maybe.'

One of the young cats comes up close, attracted by my game of squashing the nettles. It is on the hunt for food. When it realises there is no food, it turns away again with a disdainful backwards flick of its face. I am shocked to see that it has pale blue eyes, not the butter yellow eyes of its brothers or sisters.

'Only maybe?'

I shrug. Perhaps I want to keep the memory - the feeling - private. Today I just want to enjoy the sunlight, the cottony clouds, the incredible richness of the blossom on the two cherry trees that stand a little deeper in the garden. I think in this moment that I can glimpse the reason why old gardeners allow some small area of wildness. Nature is a tart here, wantonly displaying her sensuality, brazenly, wonderfully, overwhelmingly.

'Would you like a cigarette?'

'I don't smoke now. It's an unhealthy habit. I used to smoke. But the nurses persuaded me to give it up.'

'Have one anyway.'

I take his cigarette, from the second packet of twenty Benson and Hedges I have bought for him. I let him hold up the dock-end of his cigarette, so I can light mine from the tip. I inhale only a little, blow the half-inhaled smoke from my mouth.

'There was something else,' I say.

'What was that?'

'He showed me something - how to catch wild creatures, butterflies, even birds.'

Harry's eyes widen, turning this new information over in his mind. I watch him transfer the stub end of his cigarette, cradling the glowing tip again in the cave of his hand. Harry is good at getting me to talk. He would have made a good mental nurse.

He asks me, 'Because they were eating the seeds?'

'No.' I blink a slow blink, thinking back. I am catching the growly richness of the Southern Irish accent. 'For no real reason.'

'He trapped them for no real reason? Garden birds? Songbirds?'

'Yeah.'

Harry is smoking again, nodding his head. The expression on his face is one of bemusement. My own cigarette rising to my lips. Hearing the traffic roar past on the road beyond the boundary wall. The world outside the flowering cherry trees. Squinting my eyes.

'How did he trap them?'

'With a bucket propped up on a stick.'

An enamelled bucket, I reflect now, remembering it again after such a long time. It was the only enamelled bucket I ever saw in my life. I am back there, remembering things as I have not remembered them in a long time. Surprised by the vividness of the visions. I can see them, smell them, taste them. My grandfather, with that look of amusement in his eyes, opening the closed ball of his hands to allow me to breathe into it, as if I were the giver of life, resuscitating a cabbage white butterfly so that it would flutter into flight. Or watching really closely the string in his hand, the pair of us hiding inside the open door of the greenhouse. My uncertain heart watching two starlings, picking out the stupid one. The first one, which is always the most daringly inquisitive. The rainbow sparks of greenish-mauve iridescence on its wing. I notice the containment in my grandfather's excitement. The patience of long experience, so he can catch at least two birds with a single manoeuvre. The tension in the string as he drops the bucket with a metal clunk. The sudden mad fluttering inside. The look of triumph on Grandad's face as he takes one bird, calms its fluttering wings, as he grips hold of the living body in one calloused hand.

'You hated him for that?'

'No. You don't understand. He didn't harm them. It was ... just to let me see them, to let me stroke them. I had never seen birds like that before. I had never been that close to them, alive in his hands.'

'Ah!' he murmured. As if Harry himself were just realising that it was the summer after the death of my father.

'Did he teach you?'
'Oh, yes.'
Unbearable now. Not wanting to remember how I probably behaved with my grandfather. The temper tantrums because I was so upset.
'You learnt to trap birds with the bucket?'
'Yes.'
It amazed me now how I had suppressed the memory of that quivering form in my two hands, the feel of feathers, the panic of wings, the biting and scratching, until I learnt how to control it, to fold the wings in smoothly with the tiny heaving body, to soothe it until it was still and quiet. Yet there it was, this real life in my hands. Those black eyes gazing back into mine. And my grandfather laughing. Laughing at me. Laughing with me.

Harry is waiting, patiently smoking.

Being clever, I think, as I look away.

He waits long enough to light up a new cigarette. It is the last one left in the packet. He offers it to me first, accepts my refusal, then lights it himself, with his hands cupped against the slight breeze.

'You said something else. You were a disappointment to him?' He speaks after he has lit it.

Old Harry! I think. He never gives up. But I answer him patiently. 'That's right,' I say.

'But you don't really want to talk about it?'

I shrug. My neck feels strangely stiff. A glimpse of myself and my mother, during that holiday in Ireland, getting up early on a Sunday morning, setting out without breakfast so she, the English Catholic, could receive Holy Communion at the eight o'clock Mass.

'You never mentioned your grandmother.'

I squint at him, not looking at me, yet reflecting my smile. Smile for smile, though at what secret transfer of information, of feeling, I am not sure.

'My grandmother had died.'
'So he was living alone?'
'That's right.'
'And now you and your mother – you had lost your father?'

I nod reflectively. Hey, Harry shouldn't be a mental nurse. He should be a bloody psychiatrist. I wish I were smoking that cigarette now, taking that cigarette to my lips, comforting myself with that cigarette as I overcome my reluctance to remember. I am so damned uncertain of so many things, I shake my head.

'He wanted you both to come and live with him?'
'Something like that.'

I am looking up at the sky. The lovely blue, summery sky. I hear the slight breeze blowing. The sweet baritone song of a blackbird. The counterpoint soprano of a bluetit. I feel the warmth of sun and the stir of the breeze on the skin of my hands, below the sleeves of my shirt. The sensation of roughness on the sweating palms of my hands, pressed against the drying bark of the old pear tree.

'You didn't want to go and live in Ireland?'
'My mother half did. She really liked the people.'
'Then it was you, the awkward young Mylie, who turned him down?'

I say nothing, but he is right. Closer even than he could possibly realise. I felt really ashamed. I felt that not only had I let down my grandfather but the memory of my father as well. It was an awful feeling. It felt like a sin, as if I had committed the worst mortal sin.

'Do you know why you refused him?'
'No.'

A thing I just felt. I didn't think at all.

'And so something happened? Something went wrong? The feeling between you suffered?'

'There didn't seem to be ... to be the same closeness.'

I still remember it now, in this moment of beauty, under the direct sunshine. Even though I was only eight years old, I remember how deeply I had disappointed him. I saw it right there in the hurt in his eyes. The estrangement. I realise now that he must have felt rejected, abandoned. The Irishman had lost both his sons to these English people, and now he must have felt that he had lost his only grandson.

Harry hesitates again. Watches a bird now, the inquisitive blackbird, rummaging under the straggly hawthorn by the boundary wall.

'You never went back to stay with him in Ireland?'

I think: *Oh, it wasn't quite as brutal as that. There were letters. Cards at Christmas and birthdays. Now and then even a slightly uncomfortable phone call.*

'No,' I say, quietly. 'We never went back.'

20

I am lying on my back, listening to the Oasis album *Be Here Now*. As I listen, I am struggling to think. Or at least I am struggling to think clearly. There is a strange new sense of wonder in me. Maybe I am suffering from too much stimulation. I think I am suffering from too much thinking. I need to rest. I need to have an hour or two without thinking about anything at all.

It is not helped by the heat.

It is incredibly warm for early May and it is bringing out the schizophrenic in people. At least that's my theory. A new schizophrenic has been admitted, a woman in her fifties, called Emma. Emma is strange even for a schizophrenic. She is totally withdrawn from life and dissociated in her mood. Nobody noticed when she stopped going to work as a packer in a plastics factory. Nobody noticed when she unscrewed the number plates from her Fiat Uno. Nobody noticed when she stopped leaving the house, when she stopped paying the bills, or when the telephone, electricity and gas supplies were cut off. Emma no longer went out to shop in the supermarket. She kept her curtains closed all day. All that kept Emma alive – and she was little more than a skeleton when she came in – was the regular bottle of milk from the milkman. It was the milkman, knocking her up to get paid for his deliveries, that saved Emma's life.

So that is what I have been doing today, specialing Emma. Doctor Mehta's interview would have been hilarious if her condition had not been so serious. I really like Doctor Mehta, although I rarely find myself working with his patients. He's a Hindu and this gives him a different outlook on life. Nothing appears to upset him. It makes me laugh the way he shakes his head from side to side when he is explaining things to his patients. Today, when I got angry about what had happened to Emma, he sat down and had a cup of tea with me in the kitchen and we talked about a belief called Kismet, which is the Hindu word for Fate. He explained how every individual life is a river, the River of Life, which finds it origins up there in the mountains between the clouds. The River may follow many twists and turns along its meandering way, but the journey always ends in the sea.

So here I am daydreaming on my bed. The music is The Verve: *Urban Hymns*. I am back on the beach in Majorca and Tabi is running in front of me, both of us out of our skulls from drinking *Tropical* beer at lunchtime at the Azzurro. The sun is almost directly above us, the hot Majorcan sun beating down hard on our bodies. We have to hop and skip over the hot white sand, stumbling like lunatics, as we stagger up the slopes of the dunes, prickly with wild flowers.

We have shouted our drunken *hasta-la-vistas* to the weasel-faced Carlos, who picks his nose in front of you while he is taking your order for food. At the Azzurro, it has to be simple. One huge plate of chips, placed centrally, fought over and devoured between our greedy fingers. Two pints of beer to begin with. Quickly, another two pints of beer. Soon we have lost track of those cool foaming pints of beer.

The select few have found their heaven here, in this hidden bay, with its ramparts of sand dunes and the horse-shoe shapes of windbreaks constructed out of old blue stone, thrown up out of the ground by the same tectonic violence that created the Alps. The violence of the Earth has evolved this protection for naked bodies.

We find a depression between dunes. The flowers, like lilac stars on the aromatic spindly stalks of thyme, are watching us as we tear off our clothes. We are making love within ten seconds. German nudists walking by, middle-aged, blubber hanging free all over the place. I can't feel her hand upon me because I am anaesthetised by the alcohol. We are convulsed with laughter, my anaesthetised state only reluctantly responding to her juddering warmth. Tabi is laughing like the waves of the sea. I mock myself with the vision of my buttocks moving. More laughter, screaming laughter. We are no longer naked. We are clothed in sand. Sand is coating our skins through the glue of our sweat. The sand is vaguely prickling on the engine of my prick, carrying the sand up Tabi's warm dark cave. I am making love to the beach. I am making love to the sea. With the whole world spinning around my head.

Magical! Oh Jesus – wonderful!

I have got to the stage where I am half-drunk on Jack Daniels, more like three-quarters drunk to be absolutely honest with you, reading the book again.

I can hear the squeals coming from across the landing, where Rich is frolicking noisily with Angie, to the mesmeric rhythms of Moby. The cannabis fumes are rising up the stairs, from where Janus is smoking away his anger at unemployment, comforting himself with throbbing beat of Destiny's Child. With tears of laughter still misting my eyes, I am returning to this relationship Rubashov has with the prisoner in cell 402. They have ridiculous conversations, using Morse code. Rubashov taps on the wall with his pince-nez. No 402 taps back with his monocle. Oh man – this familiar desperation really cracks me up, this sparring across the wall with the pince-nez and the monocle. This really kills me. This mysterious stranger, who you never get to meet, tells Rubashov that it serves him right to land up in prison. I agree with him. I really do. Rubashov has been a right old fruit-and-nut case in his time. It seems that they are traditional enemies of some sort, although they have never met in life. In between pacing up and down his cell and suffering from toothache, Rubashov amuses himself by guessing what 402 looks like – and then he keeps changing his mind.

Of course I realise that something important is happening, something complex beyond the script. I am talking about the script of life, which should tell you how wild is the direction in which I am heading.

Harry and me, we're back in the garden again. We have counted two more feral cats. So the family, including both parents – the father is the same white as three of the four young ones, only bigger and more mangy looking – amounts to six. Actually they look surprisingly well fed, the younger brood - sleek and fit.

'Don't ever grow old,' says Harry, with half a smile. 'Everything goes bad on you. You get warts growing on your skin.'

It is hot enough for us to wear open-necked shirts and even then to sweat in them, here, in the place we are beginning to think of as the "Abandoned Garden". Harry is grumbling away there, rubbing at some warty patches on the skin of his arm. He says, with that same peculiar half-grin, 'I told you that I like Yorkshire.'

No way has he told me anything of the kind. What Harry told me, once, when he was winding me up, was he knew Yorkshire. Like he knew Sheffield – "The Independent Socialist Republic!" I don't contradict him.

Under our feet, the grass and the soil is swarming with ladybirds. There are so many of them you think of a flood - an invading tide of ladybirds caused by the heat. The blossom is so luscious, so luxuriant, it appears to be weighing down the branches of the cherry trees. The pink petals are carpeting the ground around our feet.

Harry is going through the ritual. Accepting the new packet from my hand – another twenty pack of Benson and Hedges I bought him. Tearing the cellophane from the golden cover. Stopping at that point for a moment. I see what is the focus for his eyes. Tiny buds of pure white blossom are starting to peep out of their young green fists, between the darker leaves of the old pear tree, on the trunk of which I am sitting, swinging one leg. It is going to be another hot and sunny afternoon.

Although he has the match ready, he doesn't finish lighting up. Not yet. A kind of alternative fire is glowing in his eyes, which are still dazed, it appears to me, by the sight of that late-opening blossom.

'You should know, being a Yorkshireman, that the regiment I joined was a Yorkshire regiment. The Green Howards.'

A blink of his eyes. Only now does he continue opening the packet, slips a cigarette out of the tightly packed cluster. He studies the box of matches. He makes a performance of reading the label. He lights the match off the coping stones, between the flowers of lichen and some petals of cherry blossom that have been trapped in the spaces between the stones.

There is a pretence at carelessness in the gesture but there is nothing careless going on here. There is nothing careless about Harry. In the ensuing silence, as he fills the tiny garden with the fragrance of the cigarette, I think about what he has just said, which puzzles me.

Like the second move in a game of chess, he continues, 'I walked into one of the recruitment offices in London and they called them up in Richmond. Paid for my fare north.'

'Why?' I ask the question that is expected of me.

He pauses, shifts his focus once more on to the branches over my head, into the scrabbly branches in the pear tree, where the pure white blossom is struggling to open into the light.

'My old man was more of a Londoner than I was. He could have called himself a real Cockney, since he was born within the sound of Bow Bells. I was born in Greenford, in Middlesex. That was his regiment, my old man - the Middlesex Regiment.'

'He wouldn't have been pleased when you joined the Green Howards?'

A pawn offered and accepted. He follows up with a readjustment of his chess pieces.

You notice a little more each time you come here. Here. In the Abandoned Garden.

There is a hole in a wall where a door once stood, confirming that the wall where Harry is smoking was once the garden wall of the old cottage, overlooking the tiny orchard and vegetable garden. The pear tree could not have grown naturally to make the seat. Hands have trained it. Hands that knew the soil and worried about the seasons. One generation for the sake of the next. Generations of families have lived here, people who did not regard themselves as Londoners. The city, much smaller in those days, would have been a day's travel by foot. Men and women in rustic clothes have sat on this tree. Men with white clay pipes between their teeth, talking calmly, discussing their worries, their hopes. Telling stories to their children. The way a family communicates things that are important to them. The way Harry is communicating now. Communicating, in that clear, gentle voice of his, eyes still dreaming amongst the branches over my head.

'I was born not twenty miles from here, in the family hotel. An old place, with black beams, on the main road into Northolt. There were reminders of the old man's regiment everywhere. Photographs of men in uniform. The old boy himself, as sharp as a weasel, in his Captain's hat. The colours. Helmets. Brasses.' A pause to inhale, to enjoy the reflection. 'His service medals took pride of place, in the centre of the wall behind the bar.' Another puff, the smoke drawn deep into Harry's lungs, doing that damage he doesn't give a damn about. 'It was all over a girl,' he says, with a shake of his head. 'A girl called Annie.'

I smile at last. It is self-driving now. I need say nothing.

In the new pause, while he gathers his thoughts about Annie, I look closer at the other wall, which meets the one on which Harry is sitting at an angle of ninety degrees.

Yeah, I am sure about it. I can make out the long stone shape of a sill, barely above ground level, that must have been the sill of the pantry window. I imagine the woman inside, peering out of the tiny opening, watching her husband digging in the vegetable garden, or watching her children playing around the tree.

A sound causes me to glance back at Harry, at the intensity of the expression that has invaded his face, unfocusing his eyes. Not anger or sadness. I think it is a look of longing.

'Annie ...' I help him out.

'She had lovely hair. Black hair.' A big inhalation into his lungs. 'Jewish black hair.'

'Annie was Jewish?'

He has surprised me again. Swinging my blue-jeaned leg backwards and forwards, over where the nettles once stood, I am watching some ants scurry about on the heated brown earth, where my treading boots have wiped out the nettles and grasses under the tree.

'A refugee', he continues, 'with a German accent. That was what made me notice her at the dance in the village hall. And the... the longing behind the sparkle of life in her eyes.'

I am beginning to see the ghost of Annie. Small and dark, the thick mop of black hair. Curly black hair. And deep brown eyes full of longing.

'On Horsenden Hill,' he says, making a liquid sound as his lips part to smile. 'I courted Annie on Horsenden Hill. I kissed her. She was what you might call a kisser. She had the lips for it. Big lips. Soft lips. Kissed you with a hunger. A need.' The old devil is chuckling to himself, remembering himself kissing Annie.

'Your first time, Harry?'

I do not say it offensively, only enviously

'No. We never went half that far. She was only fifteen, going on sixteen. I was sixteen, going on seventeen.'

Jesus, but I'm more envious than ever! I'm half way to being horny thinking about Harry aged sixteen, having his first fumbles through the tight layers of Annie's clothes. In the grass. Up there, on Horsenden Hill.

'It was my jungle. I played there as far back as I can remember. The hill was 365 feet high, exactly. There was a plaque on the top of it that told you that. The Grand Union Canal ran through it, through one side of it. We played cowboys and Indians, stole blackbirds' eggs out of their nests, fell out of trees. There was the place we called the haunted house. A tumbledown old place that was so overgrown you could hardly walk through it. A frightening place for children because it was so overgrown. These days it would be cleaned up.'

I help myself to a cigarette from the packet he has placed on the wall next to where he is sitting. I light up, scratching the match as he has scratched his match, as a hundred years of men have scratched, over the lichened surface of the stone.

'You took her there, to the haunted house, to frighten her first?'

'Of course,' he laughs. 'Little Annie – my first girl. I adored her the way you adore your first girl.'

'You randy devil!' I inhale enough to damage my own lungs, with a feeling of guilt that Harry does not share.

'Horsenden Hill!' Shaking his head. 'It was so high in the winter you got enough snow to toboggan down it. I remember one or two people being killed coming down there – on their wooden toboggans, straight into the trees.'

On wooden toboggans, I reflect, that their fathers would have made for them. Harry's toboggan, made for him by his war-gassed father?

'What was his name, your father?'

'Edward.'

Teddy, I notice that. Teddy. Like Harry's son.

'It was the long summer holidays. Back from school. The last long vacation. The following year I would be taking my National Certificate.'

'You went to boarding school, then?'

'A minor public school. The same school my father attended.' Harry's voice becoming more clipped, not interested in talking about the school. 'Later on I discovered that my father had a friend called Simon Barnstable, who was half Jewish himself. He told the old man that if she became pregnant I would have to become a Jew and marry her.'

We smoke for a while in silence, Harry waiting for me to arrive at the inevitable conclusion.

'So they broke it up? This romance between you and the Jewish refugee girl called Annie?'

'They were all against it. There was a lot of prejudice in those days. They were worried I would have to become a Jew.' Harry looking up into the leaves of the old pear tree, over my head. At the small white fists of opening blossoms.

'Would you have become a Jew and married her?'

'I don't know – maybe I would. I think I would have done anything for Annie.'

I have never heard Harry talk like this before. So freely. To appear to enjoy the very act of talking.

'What did they do?'

'They packed my bags and sent me away, to my mother's people. In Brandon.'

In the ensuing silence, I discover the need to stretch my legs. I stub out my cigarette on the paving stones next to the wheelchair, where it rests close to the wall. I hesitate, pick up the extinguished cigarette and put it into my pocket. Glance once more at the wheelchair. It will be redundant soon, when Harry finishes his course of ECT. I pace the worn path as far as the boundary wall. I can hear the roar of the traffic off to my right, on the hot tarmac road that is another world.

I know what he is going to say before he says it. There is such an intensity of communication between us, I don't want it to end.

'I missed Annie terribly,' his voice carries across to me. 'I suppose that I truly loved her, even the foreignness about her. Perhaps especially the foreignness. All that she had gone through. It wasn't surprising that she was always so damned nervous. But you could see it - see it there. Her needing me too. In the longing in her eyes.'

I realise something really startling. Something wonderful. Whatever is important to you – whatever is really important – is actually so simple.

The realisation is so intensely moving, I have to look away, turn off my mind. I gaze at what has been obvious from the beginning: that the cherry trees are young, new. So they had to have been planted by the gardener we had seen. Why? Perhaps he had some left over from planting in the grounds? Perhaps he had no garden at home? Perhaps for other reasons I didn't know.

Harry is talking about this place called Brandon, but I am only half listening. Some place I never heard of, in rural Suffolk. The way his hotel-owning family had used the excuse of the Blitz. The local air-raid shelter was flooded and his mother couldn't sleep at night, worrying about his safety. I am thinking about Annie. About Harry, aged sixteen, and Annie, aged fifteen. On the green hill that had been his playground since as far back as he can remember. He catches my attention again, talking about his Uncle Charlie. There is a sudden animation, a real warmth of affection in Harry, when he talks about his Uncle Charlie.

'You see, Charlie was the scallywag of the family. He loved trains.'

'Trains?'

'Yes – trains. He kept running away from boarding school so he could go and watch the trains. He gave it all up to become a railway signalman at a place called Little Port in the Fens.'

'A railway signalman,' I murmur, smiling.

'Oh – but he wasn't an idle fellow, Charlie! He had a good brain and wanted something to do with it, something to keep him thinking, when he wasn't pulling levers or working the gates or whatever.'

'So what did he do, this Uncle Charlie?' I am back on my perch on the old pear tree.

'With Charlie, it had to be daring. Perhaps he envied my father his success with the hotel. Anyway, he had it in his mind to earn some money. And he did it too. He ended up quite wealthy, for a signalman.'

Harry is offering me the packet of Benson and Hedges. I am still trying to picture this character, Uncle Charlie, as Harry strikes the match for me, cradling my face in the bowl of his hands.

'Well – he borrowed some money to buy a smallholding. He set up his greenhouses there, on the smallholding. He grew tomatoes for the market.' I am laughing with Harry, his laughter is so infectious. 'He was the shrewdest fellow I ever met. You see, he knew when the trains were coming and he had a little car, a Morris, and he would trundle around the Fens, in between trains.'

'How do you mean, in between trains?'

'Oh, nothing was too daring for Uncle Charlie. He would leave his box and clear off in the car. He knew he had an hour until the next train came or an hour and twenty minutes, or whatever. So off we would go, the pair of us, and we'd meet up with this smallholder or farmer in a field. We would walk up and down the field and he'd pick a few of this and a little of that and the other, and he'd say I'll give you twenty-five quid a ton.'

We are laughing again. Smoking together.

'So then he started to buy the fields. Whole fields. They'd be growing carrots, peas, parsnips – whatever. He'd get people in to pick them and then he'd have them shipped from the little yard outside his box to these wholesalers in London. Free of charge. By train.'

Harry is suddenly roaring with laughter. We are both laughing until there are tears in our eyes.

'I was appointed his chief melon sniffer. He decided – and this was the war remember, with all of the rationing and whatever – he decided he would grow cantaloupe melons in his cold frames. They were very difficult to come by, of course, so he could make a few bob on them. But you had to get them when they were just about to ripen. And because I was staying with him it was easier to put me in one end of the cold frame and let me crawl down to the other end. It was quite a distance, and along the way I had to sniff the melons to see if they were approaching ripeness. You could tell those that were becoming ripe because of the sweet smell. One day over and they opened up like a rose and were useless for the market, they split into thick segments, right round the stalk. Uncle Charlie was always accusing me of deliberately missing one, because I had a constant supply of melons.'

I could see it, though the renewed laughter. I could see Harry, aged seventeen, sneaking back to the cold frames to get hold of the cantaloupe he had put aside for himself. Finding his reward with his nose, the sweetness of it, getting the luscious fruit all over his face as he trudged homewards down the mile or two of isolated track to the signalman's cottage.

Listening to Harry, I sense it now, I sense it so strongly. I sense it through the tears of laughter, that Harry is not telling me all of the truth. And this is a place where the first rule is the truth. Here it must be told, openly and honestly. I see, feel, taste, hear, digest this law of rightness. It is so overwhelming that I don't quite understand it for a minute or two. And then understanding floods in, in a tidal wave of wonder.

'You did it. You went all the way with her, didn't you?'

'What is the world coming to, when ...'
'Don't bullshit me, Harry.'
There can be no lies here in the Abandoned Garden. There must be no secrets, here, no matter how dark. Here, already, we have started the process. We are past the beginning, with all this gentle talk about childhood. Here, under the falling cherry blossom and the hard struggle into a new year of life for the old pear tree, there is an obligation on both of us to tell the truth. Here we have started to strip the flesh from the bones.

'We made love.'

The words rise up out of the heart of him, in a croak of delight. I can see the languor of it in his glowing eyes. Like that time for me with Alison Morley, my loss of virginity against the wall in the rain.

For a long time neither of us speaks. I hear the sound of bees in the jumble of flowers by the corner. A cabbage white butterfly flutters around the branches, as if annoyed that the pear blossom isn't yet open.

'Did you ever hear more about Annie?'

'After my certificate, when I came back home from school for the last time. It was 1944, just a few months before my call-up papers. We couldn't sleep in the bomb shelter, it was so flooded. I'd have had to learn to swim. So we lay awake on the mattresses between the barrels of beer in our cellar and we listened to the doodlebugs. One day we heard one roar straight over our heads. It went into a block of flats in Harrow.'

He is quiet now, thoughtful for a few seconds.

'My sister told me about her. She talked about Annie when she felt frightened by the doodlebug. She told me that Annie's parents were desperate. They had no job and no money. The place was full of Americans. She told me how they sent Annie out on to the streets. So they could live off her immoral earnings.'

'Oh Jesus!'

'Of course I refused to believe her. I didn't want to believe her. Yet still I went off to war, wondering what part I had played in that. Not knowing if my sister was lying to me, to make me feel guilty.'

'If she was lying, it was a pretty mean trick to play on you.'

'Yes.' Harry's eyes have returned to that unfocused stare. His gaze has returned to the branches over my head.

21

It is the patients, I think, who are keeping me sane.

I was watching Jock doing his Tai Chi exercises. You would have to see him doing his exercises to believe it. He is tall and angular to start with. Then he takes up a pose that reminds you of two mating storks. His arms are the necks and his hands, with his fingers flexed against the tips of his thumbs, are the heads. I watch how the mating ritual develops. Sometimes he extends them to his maximum reach, along precise diagonals in his sense of the three-dimensional geometry between earth and sky. The hands are the hovering beaks, facing each other, ready to meet. They make sharp jerks towards each other, with his whole gaunt body stretched taut, like a wire. Or he will pose with his two clenched fists above his head, fingers outermost and the long white thumbs extended upright. Then he bends over the whole of his body from the waist and very slowly turns in a circle, doing jerks with his neck and letting go of little puffs of breath, so he sounds exactly like a steam train hissing.

I have rooted through the three thick volumes of Jock's notes, which tabulate his long-term illness. What I have discovered is a diagnosis, right at the beginning, from a psychiatrist called Dr C.J. Wells, who labelled Jock's original illness as a chronic anxiety state. So Jock and the Reverend Peter are each suffering from a very similar kind of illness, a chronic anxiety state. In Peter's case it shows up as obsessional-compulsive behaviour while in Jock's case it appears to be an inability to rest, a desperate passion to keep moving, always moving.

Isn't it just incredible how something we all recognise as simple nervousness, this condition the psychiatrists call anxiety, could so profoundly take hold of two intelligent human lives?

Then, just after lunch today, I overheard a conversation between the Reverend Peter and Alice.

Actually, Peter is showing a lot of improvement. The clockwork mechanism is righting itself in his head. He is still shouting down the corridors, of course, but mainly just 'shit' and 'piss' these days. But still he feels depressed because of the time it is taking. Because when you start to improve, you get impatient about the length of time it takes to get better.

That was why Alice came up and comforted him. 'We all drops of water in de ocean!' she said, putting her arm around his shoulders.

'Yes, Al-Al-Al-ice!' he stammered. 'B-but all those drops make up the ocean. And if you analyse a single drop, you know the ocean.'

I am rushed off my feet at work these days on the wards. I am busy out of my skin, sweating away in the continuing heat. The television and newspapers are doing calculations about global warming. A few weeks ago, central England was washed away with floods followed by snow, but now they are projecting that if the mean temperature rises just one more degree, France and Spain will be deserts and the south of England will have a Mediterranean climate.

But I can't afford the time to worry about all that. What I am really worrying about all the time is Harry – Harry, who has had the fourth of his ECT therapies. I know there was that initial improvement. It was very encouraging, that initial improvement. Enough to get him out into the grounds. Enough to let him talk to me. But there has to be more. Harry is not going to survive unless there is more, but I haven't seen much evidence of it yet. I haven't seen enough improvement to make me think that he is going to make it. Not compared with the sort of progress you see in other patients. So it is little wonder I am wandering around in a day dream, hearing Shola Ama in my head - Shola Ama, who is Tabi's favourite singer. I am haunted by Shola Ama, singing 'You Might Need Somebody' in my head.

I would like to think that Harry is a bit more optimistic, following the ECT. I know that he is getting excited about Claudia going to see Muriel. Getting his hopes up.

I tried to find a few minutes after the breakfasts to talk to him, because I could see he was really uptight since yesterday. He was getting himself all worked up. He hadn't touched his breakfast at all and I tried to get him to eat just a piece of toast.

'No news about Muriel?'

He shook his head.

The house that Harry shared with Muriel is miles away from the hospital, in the far north of London. A little place near Buckhurst Hill. I have never been there. I have never even heard of it, to tell you the truth. I only know about it because I have been taking another look at Harry's medical notes. And those notes have been proliferating. So I know from those notes that Grumpy is doing his best for Harry. He has been taking Harry through a series of deep psychoanalytical sessions. I can see, from Grumpy's notes, that the trouble with Muriel has been going on for years. The business with his dog, Nobby, was just the last straw in the breakdown of the relationship between Harry and Muriel. And Harry is now blaming himself for this.

'It was mostly my fault,' he said to me today, with a forlorn expression on his face.

I have to accept that I was the one who set this ball rolling. I mean, I was the one who asked Harry about Muriel. But it was a bit embarrassing when he started talking so bluntly about their sexual relationship.

He said, 'Even an old woman like Muriel needs a little physical comforting now and then. A little getting together. You lose them when you stop giving them that comfort.'

Hey, Harry – thanks for that little piece of practical advice!

All the same I keep pestering Claudia for news. Claudia is good at her job. You have to put aside the notion of her being screwed by Boyson. I mean, you haven't seen Claudia when she is stoking up. I'm telling you! When I read that old book *Brave New World*, I never understood what Huxley meant when he described some woman as pneumatic. But when I see Claudia all worked up, I get a different picture. She has this lower lip that makes you think pneumatic. A red-blooded heterosexual male sees a lip like that and he feels the irresistible force of horny expectation. Of course it could be that almost a year of abstinence is having its effects on me.

All right – okay! So I'm feeling the pressure right now. I am feeling the heat.

I am also mad as hell with Claudia because I know that she has been to see Muriel more than once, and nothing useful has come of these visits. I know this because Claudia has talked to Grumpy after each visit. I'll tell you the real reason I'm mad with her: I suspect she is giving in to these liberal notions of Boyson's. I wonder if she doesn't push Muriel all that much because she believes it is a matter of choice whether Muriel comes in to see Harry or she doesn't. I wonder if she understands that forgiveness is a matter of life and death to Harry.

This mutual level of understanding – that's the really fantastic thing that has evolved all by itself. We never talk about the ordinary things. The ordinary things we talk about while Harry is still on the ward. Here, in the Abandoned Garden, it is as if some spell is winding itself around us, drawing us deeper into magical matters, a spell about the other things maybe, the things we are too embarrassed to talk about in ordinary life, like hope and love and despair.

I am drowning in this magical place. I am drowning in this garden of spells.

I sense it more powerfully than ever – that fathers have talked to sons here. Mothers to daughters. Mothers to sons and fathers to daughters. Every conversation a little bit special and yet the same.

How many times? I wonder. How many generations?

I mean, here we are, by half past two, sitting opposite each other, Harry on the wall and me on the old pear tree – which has struggled into a very creditable blossom, considering its dotage. That is when I kick myself because I haven't thought of asking him about music. It is Harry himself who starts talking about music. About the kinds of music he liked back in those good old days. Then, all of a sudden, he is talking about the big band forties and ragtime jazz. I find myself just shaking my head in a state of shock. I feel so stupid because I would have thought he was more Mantovani and the Proms, to be honest with you.

I am listening to him talking away about the fifties and the way rock'n'roll spoiled it for people like himself and his wife, Elizabeth, because they were into old-fashioned ballroom dancing. It is the first time he has ever opened up about Elizabeth since that time he mentioned her on the ward. I am staggered to discover the importance of dancing to Harry. And now, suddenly, I think back and I realise that I mentioned Tabi and her love of dancing to him. I realise that I talked about her dancing back then – at much the same time he first mentioned Elizabeth and Teddy to me. Talk about going round in circles!

Anyway, I was interested to hear that he and Elizabeth had won prizes for ballroom dancing in England as well as in Rhodesia, where, as I now gather, they met for the first time.

It was the first thing to come out of all that war and rationing, which is what he is now explaining to me.

It wasn't the war really, because people discovered a way of getting together they never found in peacetime, he explains. It was the rationing and the grey cloud of deprivation that hung over everything. And then things got really swinging.

You would believe him too, if you could see the way his eyes are lighting up. So, it occurs to me, that that was how Harry pulled the birds.

From the way he is talking, I can tell that he was good at it. He was hot stuff when it came to that old-time ballroom dancing.

'Oh yes!' he replies when I ask him. 'It just came naturally to me.' He says this with a wink. It is the first time I have ever seen Harry wink.

Old Harry, so full of surprises!

He says with a grin, 'It was a talent I just found I had when I was about fourteen years old and I started hanging around the church halls in Greenford.'

Yeah, but it's nice listening to Harry talk about the dancing. I know I shouldn't but I find myself accepting another of his cigarettes – mine really, since I am the only one on the Unit willing to bring them in for him –

and I am back into this addictive and unhealthy habit again, half closing my eyes, trying to visualise it.

Only then do I miss the cats. The cats are off somewhere else today - hunting or, more likely, begging. The Garden seems to miss them though. It seems less interesting without them.

'I even tried to make my living out of it.' Harry is really getting into it now, talking about the dancing. 'After the army. When I returned to civvies.'

'What? Become a professional dancer?'

I am so surprised by this, I am positively intrigued by this, coming back to the tree to sit down after a few minutes of roaming around.

'People told me I was better than the professionals. But I didn't want to go into that. I set up my own thing. Organised dances in clubs and hotels. Teaching young people. I'd take the floor with Elizabeth, or one of my pupils, to get them going.'

'Wow!'

But he doesn't elaborate. There is a bit of a silence at this point, to tell you the truth. So the dancing lessons, the evenings in the ballrooms of clubs and hotels, didn't work out.

I reflect for a moment or two on this. On how a much younger Harry would have coped with that failure.

There would have been rows, knowing the little I know about Harry. The beginning of the end with Elizabeth is what I am wondering about. And that is when our eyes meet, which is not so unusual with Harry any more, but I know that something is coming. Something else. Something that is going to rock the boat of this pleasant afternoon.

I can guess at what is coming, because it has been a long time coming. Harry is going back again to talk about the war.

I murmur, 'You don't have to talk about it. You don't have to go upsetting yourself.'

He is shaking his head. 'I have to talk about it. I have to tell somebody.'

'Well, it doesn't have to be today, Harry.'

His voice has gone suddenly dry. He croaks to me, in this husky kind of voice, 'Maybe you could find me a drink of water, Mylie?'

I find a brass tap on a standpipe in the gardener's yard. But there isn't a cup or anything so I have to go around and knock on the door of the greenhouse, where I find the gardener working. He is lifting seedlings off the shelves, picking them up in some flat wooden trays, hundreds of pale green seedlings all pricked out in rows, and carrying two trays at a time out into his trailer barrow. I startle him with my sudden appearance. Then he finds me a battered old mug, with a pattern of strawberries and bright green leaves on it. There are chips off around the rim and the bowl inside is a web of tiny cracks. I fill it to the brim with ice-cold water from the standpipe and I take it, slopping water here and there on the broken path, through into the Garden for Harry.

'I had a friend,' he says, 'a very good friend, in the Green Howards. He was Welsh, from one of the little mining towns in South Wales. One of those first names you couldn't pronounce, Yiyean it sounded like, or something like that. We called him Froggy Pritchard.'

I know all this. He has mentioned Froggy Pritchard before. But I don't interrupt him.

'The Green Howards is a Yorkshire Regiment. You know that.'

Yeah, Harry, I know this too. The old duffer repeating himself again. I swipe out in irritation at a bluebottle that is trying to feed off the sweat on my face.

I ask him, 'But why would you do that, Harry? There must have been a dozen regiments in or around London.'

'Like the Middlesex, you mean?'

'That's right.'

And then I sigh, because I am beginning to understand. 'You did it to spite your old man.'

'Maybe.'

'Because of Annie?'

A sudden tension. It is unbelievable. I mean we are talking about the Stone Age here, but there is Harry, his eyes glittering, nodding.

A hesitation while he sips at his water. Suddenly a number of tumblers are falling in my mind. Like his Uncle Charlie before him, Harry had abandoned the family tradition. Harry, the rebel, had run away from his father's regiment to become a squaddie in the Green Howards. In the Middlesex, they'd have made him into an officer. Just like his father, the Captain.

'Why Froggy? Why did they call your mate, Froggy?'

'He was five foot three, with his feet sticking out to either side when he walked.' Harry laughs, doing a little imitation of his feet sticking out almost sideways. 'Like Charlie Chaplin,' he says. 'Some people are born to play the clown. Froggy had a face that was broader than it was long. With a wide mouth and thick lips, and a big deep voice. When you heard his voice you couldn't believe the little man it came out of. Not until you heard him sing.'

'He was a singer?'

'Oh, beautiful! A beautiful bass singer, was Froggy. He could out-do Paul Robeson singing 'Deep River' or 'Only God Can Make a Tree'.' Harry chuckling to himself, having another swig at his water. 'He'd be drunk as a lord within an hour of hitting the NAAFI. Needed to get drunk, you see, to get up the courage to go on the stage. Then he'd sing a mixture - Robeson, Welsh hymns and the vilest rugby songs you have ever heard. He was very popular.'

Yeah! I could imagine he was.

Harry has put down the mug and he is trying to light his cigarette. His hands are trembling so much I have to help him light the cigarette.

'He ... Froggy ... he ... ' Tears have begun to well up in Harry's eyes. He is getting himself so worked up.

'That's it, Harry,' I say, firmly. 'I don't want to hear any more about the war. I'm not going to listen to it.'

'Well, it was you who asked me.' It is his turn to be angry with me, to be aggressive with me in his turn.

'I never asked you to talk about the war.'

'You asked about Richard Giles,' he replies, urgently now, his voice hardly above a whisper.

I have forgotten about that in the heat of the moment. Now I am baffled by it. I am stunned into silence.

'You asked me about his name in the book.'

I get up from the tree and I walk a few paces down the garden. I am eaten up by restlessness. I know that Harry must stop here. I want him to stop it, to stop talking about the war altogether. It is getting me every bit as upset as it is Harry.

I take my time, having a peep at the wasps' nest I have discovered in an overgrown ivy patch. I have noticed there are several varieties of bees and wasps buzzing around the Garden. Little hover wasps that come up close to your face to have a look at you. Big heavy bumblebees, that bounce off walls, like cannon balls. Now I stare at this humming frenzy, at the angry stripes of their tiny bodies, as they buzz in and out.

'The irony is,' he has recovered himself and is talking calmly, normally, again, 'I didn't need to go at all. My Uncle Charlie – he could have arranged things. A safe job at home that was vital to the war effort. I could have been apprenticed to a shire horse.'

I don't know how to respond. It reminds me of the old situation. I know that Harry is once again figuring me out, sizing me up. Although his vision is on the blossom on the pear tree.

'Apprenticed to a shire horse?'

It is a relief for the moment to get Harry away from talking about the war. I allow silence to manoeuvre him back to his tales about his Uncle Charlie, the signal-box man, who lived in Brandon in the wilds of Suffolk.

22

The cherry blossom is just about done, the last few petals falling with the slightest breeze. It is lying in a pink decaying carpet all over and around the low wall, and blowing all about us where we are sitting. Some petals have fallen on to the feral cats, where they lie curled in a ball in the shade of the pear tree, all six of them in a tousled litter, asleep, with slitted eyes. I notice the way they close their eyes, not just with the fall of eyelids, but with an infolding of their entire face. They fold their faces down into slits that merge in their perfect curves with the wedge of their snouts. All embracing. Jealous for each other's warmth, the soft intimacy of each other's touch. Only the raised up ears alert, pinkly alert, are occasionally flicking.

'I don't find it easy to talk about things ... certain things.'

Harry is silent. He asks no questions. But the truth is there, in the fine, gentle tension between us.

That, based on my new level of understanding, there are things we are now sharing that we never planned to share. Things we hate to share. With me, it is Tabi. With Harry it is not Muriel, or Elizabeth, or Teddy. With Harry it is the war.

'Yeah,' I murmur, slurring the word. Slurring it lazily, self-indulgently. Sitting on my perch in the dappled shade. Wondering whether to do a bit of strolling around, to check things out, to peer at a cluster of stubborn pear blossom on which a bee or a butterfly is feeding. To check out the wasps, or the bees buzzing about the newly opened purple heads of the untended chives. Instead I do nothing. I just sit there, swinging one leg, on the tree.

This is the game I play. I give people time. The way I have been giving Tabi time. The way, right now, I am giving Harry time. I can see that he is working out in his bewildered brain just what might be on my mind.

Something to do with girls and screwing, he thinks.

I know. I can read his mind.

With Mylie everything has to do with screwing. And the truth of the matter is that Harry is right. Still, he is listening now. Listening with the third ear each of us has grown here in the Abandoned Garden.

We do not talk about the way that Muriel's continuing silence is affecting Harry - Harry, who has endured his fifth session of lightning therapy. But I can read it in his eyes. In that first faint smell about him again, which I noticed earlier, when I first stepped into his room on William Blake.

Okay, so I am telling myself to calm down. I hear the voice of my friend, Rich: *Cool it, will ya, Mylie!*

So how do I even begin to explain? That Tabi was different, special? Everybody in this world must think the same. Every man has had his Tabi – his Annie. I have to ponder this to get this right. I have to ask myself why I am even considering talking about it. I have to probe his silence. Even though I know him so well that I can interpret his silences. His silence, now, is the silence of respect.

Because each of us knows that when you enter one of those sacred places, those places of understanding, when you open up its sacred nature to another human being, it is an act of blasphemy. Yet these acts of blasphemy are where all the paths have been leading us.

Even thinking now about what I am going to tell him, knowing what I am going to confess to him, cuts down into my soul like a blade honed out of the darkest night. I steel myself with understanding. I have worked it out that this has to be the price. I know now that where my secret place is a place of joy and wonder, Harry's is a place of demons. We cannot help this. This has been the nature of our lives. There is no doubt in my mind that Harry is carrying a demon inside him. And I am the carer. It is my job as carer to exorcise this demon from the soul of my friend Harry. It is my job to set Harry free.

'When you meet Tabi for the first time you might think that she is shy. She isn't really – not shy. Or I think that shyness is probably not the word. What she is, I suppose, is truly distant.

I pause, seeing it. I am seeing that look of Tabi's in my mind.

I can't hide the strain in my voice. I feel a torment of heat on my face. If I look towards him, if I face the eyes of Harry, I will be looking into the sun. My head falls to a more shaded position.

'There is this look, sometimes, in her eyes, as if they were too big and too grey – too unfocused. As if she never has more than half her attention on what is happening around her, which makes you wonder where the other half of her attention is.'

He has lit a cigarette, and I can smell the smoke. He is waiting the way a friend will wait. He is indulging me, waiting patiently.

'We'd get back to her house and run up the stairs to her room. It's a big old rambling kind of house, with a curling staircase, and my hand would be rapping on the banisters as we were running, as if I was beating time to reach her bedroom. Our clothes would be climbing off our backs before we hit the bed or the carpet or the wall, in between the black and whites of James Dean and the one huge colour poster from the Disney film *Fantasia*.'

Time loosening up in the membranes of my mind. Time is draining away. I can feel it, the sliding, shimmering motion of it.

'I suppose', I stir, move my hand in the dream of memory, hear my disembodied voice talking, 'it was just like turning the key and opening the door into... into this place that was another Garden.'

Somebody less sensitive than Harry might laugh, mock what I am trying to explain. But Harry does not laugh or mock.

'We were each as bad as the other, the way we kept pushing it further, wanting it with a hunger that could never be entirely satisfied except by pushing it harder, further still.'

I hesitate, close my eyes, close them up tight altogether. I am cutting deep now. I am feeling the pain.

'I didn't know how to handle it, Harry. I was out of my depth. I had to cover it up, to hide the fact I was so out of my depth.' I have to hesitate, sucking in whole lungfuls of air. I wonder if it is possible to drown in air. 'I laughed at her. That first time. It nearly broke us up. It nearly ended it all, in that stupid moment, when the mocking grin invaded my face.'

It isn't a conversation. Even the memory is closer to what a child feels, senses, thrills, at the sight of a butterfly: the hesitant flight, the brilliant colours of its wings.

I feel so damned uncomfortable again, even now, telling him this. The feeling surges. I have to take a step back, mentally, to rein in the adrenaline.

I notice that I am bathed in sweat, recalling the memory of it. Something I knew I had glimpsed in the agony and the wonder of it. The little girl, with her Teddy bears in her bed. The evolution, during that single clumsy encounter, into the grown woman. A female thing. Femaleness.

I pause to take my handkerchief from my pocket, to wipe my brow and face.

'I'm not a romantic person. But it was obvious to me that she wanted me to believe in some romantic image of her as she had to believe in some romantic image she had of me. She really needed this make-believe. And so I expanded myself a little bit here and pulled myself in a little bit somewhere else and I became the romantic figure that she was looking for.'

Silence now. Silence while I recover for a few moments. A pained silence until Harry clears his throat.

He speaks quietly, thoughtfully, 'It was a dream, Mylie.'

'Yeah,' I reply, 'it was a dream. But I got to the stage where I was living the dream. I got to the stage where I didn't want what was real any more. I didn't care about anything that had happened before Tabi and I got together. Only this dream world existed for me. It was like discovering the real secret language of love, behind all the touches and the kisses... and the loving.'

I should stop there, but I can't. I am struggling to surface here, but I don't want to surface. Again, I am wiping down my face.

'Jesus, Harry, I'm telling you – it was frightening. It was how I would imagine it must be when a blind person is enabled to see for the first time. You can't be half-hearted about a thing like that. You have to give yourself up to it, allow it to eat you up, body and soul, until you know that nothing of your ordinary life matters any more.'

We seem to have been talking for a long time, so long that the sun has moved and the light is falling down in dancing motes through the leaves and the blossom on to Harry's head.

I look over into the dappled face of Harry, who is sitting there with his hands lying open on his lap. He is utterly still, except for his eyes. In his eyes I am astonished by the animation of a pure blue light, as blue as a morning sky, but quick and alive, like the reflection of that blue morning sky on dappled water.

23

'Did you manage to see the woman?'

'Which woman is that, Harry?'

'Not the one who makes clay balls into a pig.'

Not Vera, who is disappointed with Harry, because he is still refusing to join her pottery classes – although I have suggested that she think about holding some kind of a dancing class, with Harry as the teacher. She is considering this. Of course I know, have known all along, that the woman Harry is referring to is Claudia. I hate this game I am playing. I am playing him out, as a fisherman plays out the fish.

'Yeah, I've seen her.'

'Did she mention Muriel?'

'No. Not yet, anyway.'

'Not yet!' he mutters. 'Not yet!'

Harry, not troubling to hide his despair, is quizzing me in the side ward.

'I'm sorry, Harry.'

'But did you ask her about Muriel?'

'She'd have told me. She knows you're waiting for news about it. She knows how anxious you are. She'd have come and told you herself, Harry.'

That awful silence then, which I just cannot do anything to prevent or to assuage. Muriel's silence becoming Harry's silence. Silence is a terrible weapon between people. A really cruel weapon.

It is a week since we last went into the Abandoned Garden. A week and neither one of us has asked the other about that. Neither of us has even referred to what was said.

His eyes glance over, his eyes pick out my eyes, as he says, 'I didn't tell you the complete truth.'

'Hey!' My voice is gentle, understanding, with him. 'There is no such thing.'

'Oh, yes there is.' His voice is a murmur. We are back once more in the murmuring phase. 'I didn't tell you the complete truth about Annie.'

I am pretending to straighten out the bedcovers. Neither Harry nor I give a damn about the bedcovers.

'What my sister told me, I already knew it wasn't the truth.'

I have to focus down, even to remember. I remember. 'Jesus, Harry! I mean, what are we talking about? We're talking about the Dark Ages here. We're talking about 1944, for Christ's sake.'

It is the wrong thing to have said. I bite my tongue because I can see the way it is upsetting him, and I have had my instructions renewed from Michael, who is increasingly worried about Harry. We are all getting increasingly worried about Harry. About the fact that he has completed the course of ECT, taken all the lightning Grumpy dares to throw at his brain, and nothing has changed. No significant improvement in the mood of this small, bald-headed man, no improvement in this thing they call his 'affect'. Harry's affect is another way of saying Harry's life-feeling. There is no point in talking about Harry's feeling of self worth, because Harry has no feeling of self-worth any more. Harry's feeling of self-worth is the same thing as his feeling of self-disgust.

You become sensitive to the rising chord of desperation in a patient's voice, its integral part in the symphony of his body movements, his eyes.

Harry is becoming desperate about Muriel, who, we all know, is never going to come.

'You don't have to talk about it. Not if it's too painful for you.'

'Isn't that the whole point of it?' he murmurs. This murmuring, which is so unconscious, it is an automaton, like the murmuring of a river or a stream, grumbling timelessly into the night.

'I think this is a mistake, Harry. I think you need to put Annie out of your head until you're feeling a bit stronger. We'll talk about it again when you feel you can cope with being upset about things.'

'Don't patronise me!'

'Who's sensitive today?'

That look again, that flicker of his eyes towards mine. 'I'm running out of time. I don't think I have it in me to wait any longer.'

I watch how he has suddenly taken to his feet and help him to sit down. He is no longer in control of his movements. His body is reacting. His body is rebelling against this pain in his spirit. Harry is sitting down there again, in his chair, his eyes drawn to the car park through the window. To the people outside, who are people and not patients.

I take him out in the wheelchair again and he jerks about in it, grumbling to himself, all the way to the Abandoned Garden. 'Come on, now!' I murmur gently, helping him out of the chair in the bright sunshine. I make sure he is secure. I help him sit down, fretfully, on the wall, Harry muttering:

'They had a one track siding for Brandon, you know, before the war. A single track that came off the main line, so the train could come in. They would leave the goods there. Most of the goods were moved on the railway – there weren't really any lorries. All they had was Arthur, the shire horse.'

I seize upon this. I encourage Harry to talk about Arthur, the shire horse.

'Yes,' he murmurs, the struggle to focus, to remember, showing clearly on his face. 'Old Arthur ... only now they used him to shunt the railway trucks containing the bombs for the bases around Norfolk. They developed that one little siding into nine or ten lines. They just arrived one day and extended the lines out like the bones of a herring, expanding them right up to the boundary of the houses. Where they had shifted fish out of Yarmouth, now they loaded bombs. They'd bring them in by train and then the lorries would come in from the RAF bases and load them up. Trains were arriving all day long, pulling the trucks that were carrying the bombs. And old Arthur would pad along, gently, patiently, all day long, moving the trucks with the bombs along the rails.'

The clarity has come back to his memories. Harry should be smiling at the clarity of his memories. I know that in his mind he is smiling. Smoking his cigarette in the cave of his hand.

'You see, that was the laugh,' he murmurs. 'I was supposed to escape down there. I went there to get away from the bombs and they were all around me, on the lorries as well as the railway trucks. Open sided trucks with straps around them, holding them in a kind of pyramid. If a bomb had landed around there, we'd have been blown to Kingdom Come, old Arthur and me.

'You see, that was when I saw the lie. Everything they had been telling me. Everything everybody has ever told me. They got rid of me to Brandon, and it was a lie.'

How can I describe the level you reach when, as a thinking human being, your voice has become an automaton, a flowing force with a will of its own, like a stream or a river? When your voice has become a conduit to some place that is beyond rationality. When your voice has become the communication to your soul. When you talk and it is without thinking, without awareness. When your voice sounds like the voice of somebody else in your own ears. When it is your soul that has had enough. When it is your soul that can no longer bear this pain.

'Her parents ...' Harry emits what could be a sigh, or it could be a moan. 'They didn't put Annie out to work the streets for them. They wouldn't have done a thing like that. She did it herself. I know – I knew then – why she did it.'

A choking sound forbids me actually looking at him. When every fibre of my caring instinct tells me to go over to him, to make sure he is all right. But if Harry is choking, it is internal. It is in his spirit that Harry is choking. In his soul.

'They kicked her out all right. I can understand why they did that, because she had got herself pregnant with a gentile. They were devout ... whatever the word is.'

Orthodox, Harry. The word is orthodox.

But I don't tell him. I dare not interrupt to say a word. I play dumb. Not noticing the cats, or what is left of the blossoms. I put myself into a clinical frame of mind. I consider how it is when people get down: they see things through a veil of gloom. They put inflections on things that were never there. They amplify old memories, cloaking them with grotesque new meanings.

'They kicked her out but they didn't make her do that. She could have got a job as a barmaid, or a shop assistant, or whatever. Any pub would have taken her, she was so damned pretty. She did that because she chose to do that. I know Annie. I know her now, better than I did then. She did that because of me.'

He covers up the choking sound by opening the packet of cigarettes. By taking his time lighting up.

'Ah, to hell with it!' he says.

I reach for the packet and take a cigarette. I smoke too. 'Yeah, Harry. To hell with it!'

'Because she loved me. Because she took the risk of loving me. And then I abandoned her.'

I have to admit that here, during these difficult days on the ward, Harry's language has been getting worse. The soldier is climbing back into his voice - the ghost from the past. I don't give a damn about that, but I feel the need to explain it, for Harry's sake. I need to explain that sometimes there is a sentence and every second word is a swear word or what in times gone by would have been a blasphemy. All I am doing is explaining it, so there is no blame, no recrimination. I am saying that it is nothing. It is nothing more than the lightning coming back out through Harry's lips.

I have finished reading the book. I have finished it at last.

It has not disappointed me. It has shocked and startled me, with these ideas that have come up out of the surface of that terrifying ocean of words.

I have thought a lot about those ideas. What the writer, Arthur Koestler, meant when he wrote them. What they might still mean for Harry.

The young cat with the white fur and the butter-yellow eyes is miaowing again, looking up into my face. Begging.

Harry's face is a mask, while he is chain smoking on his wall. 'In the LCA,' he says, 'Froggy cracked a joke. He couldn't help himself. We had been told to keep quiet, but he had to crack his joke.'

I struggle to surface from my own dreamy state to discover that Harry is laughing, the way you laugh when there are tears behind your eyes. LCA, I wonder – some kind of landing craft?

The bees buzz and butterflies flutter in and out of the fading blossom. Today is the day for butterflies. The blossom is decaying, even on the old pear tree: the blossom that, for some reason, Harry cannot take his eyes off. Harry speaking quietly, calmly, now.

I am there with Harry as he tells me about it, the flow of communication is so lucid, so clear.

'For the most part we didn't talk to each other. We were all feeling scared witless. The invasion army was the biggest ever in history. Everywhere you looked, the horizon was boiling with ships. The whole sea was taken up with tanks, armoured cars, artillery pieces, and us – thirty-odd men in a skip with a door to hell.'

A pause to light a new cigarette off the dock-end of the last one.

'You could smell the rum and minced up liver because people were puking it up. They gave us rum and minced up liver when we were waiting on board the ship. We had to wait a whole day for the storms to settle. We couldn't sleep in those sailor's hammocks so we spent the night up on deck, watching the flashes in the sky that were our bombers pounding the coastal batteries.

'The LCAs were up on davits. We didn't have to go down the scrambling nets. We climbed on board them, about thirty of us to each tin can, when they were still hanging from the davits, and then they lowered us down on cranes straight into the sea when we were still about seven miles out. Down into the water where we had to huddle down, sick as dogs, keeping our heads below the gunwales, waiting for some kind of attack, artillery or aircraft. But it never came.'

A deep inhalation of smoke. It trickles back, out of his mouth, his nostrils, the cigarette already two thirds consumed, small enough for him to reverse it so the glowing tip is now in the palm.

He puts on the deep, growly voice, with an attempt at a Welsh accent.

'Never you mind, Larry, boyo! If you don't make it, I promise I'll go back home and give your missus that shag you promised her.'

Harry creasing himself, laughing. Thinking back to his wartime friend, the other non-Yorkshireman among the Green Howards Regiment. Froggy Pritchard.

'What it was, you see – Larry had been one of the lucky ones. They gave him forty-eight hours compassionate leave. We knew it was because he had been putting his pining letters into white envelopes instead of the green ones that were designated personal. We knew he put them into white envelopes, knowing they would be opened. So the Company Office would know he was pining for Mabel. Larry had only been married to Mabel for a few months before we sailed but he had managed to get her pregnant. Froggy and I, we were jealous. We were jealous of Larry with his pining for Mabel, and it made us a lot more jealous when the Company Office sent him back for a final goodbye while we had to stay behind and sweat. And we were still sweating in the LCA at about four in the morning, when they dropped us into the sea. Every one of us had this terrible fear that the bow doors would drop down and we would be exposed, like rats caught in a trap. A single shell, a burst of machine-gun fire, and we were stuffed, before we ever got on to the beach.'

Harry is sweating copiously. His eyes are glittering as if the very pupils in his eyes are also sweating.

'Poor Larry got himself so worked up about it, he jumped out as soon as the bow door fell. But it was premature. We'd just struck the lip of a shell-hole. He jumped into ten feet of water, weighed down with the full weight of his kit. He drowned.'

Harry smoking. A single puff is about a sixth of his cigarette.

'Larry was the first to die, before the rest of us even got into the water.

'We expected air attacks, but there weren't any. Even on the beach, we got off lightly. There was a real mess of landing craft, tanks, guns, jeeps. Some had already been hit. Some were on fire. But it was going well for us. We held on there for a while, while the sappers cut the wire and found a path through the mines.

'Then, moving inland, we marched along a road. We met our first civilians. I remember a hill, with houses on the right. People coming out to meet us, offering us glasses of cider. I remember handing out sweets, handing out fistfuls of sweets to children.

'Then I saw what happened to our tanks. I saw a tank come out of cover and advance across an open field. It received a direct hit. I saw how it went up in flames. The Germans were so well hidden, their tanks or self-propelled guns, it was impossible even to see where they were firing from. I saw a second tank go through the same business. I watched it go up in flames. Then a third ...

'We started to lose people to snipers. You had to leave people in terrible pain, dying, screaming. The first time it came as an absolute shock. It was a fellow I knew, only I couldn't remember his name. I could remember that he stuttered in a Yorkshire accent, but his name just went out of my head. Shot in a ditch by a sniper. He put his head up out of the ditch and a sniper shot him through his left eye. He didn't make a sound, just fell backwards.

'The bullet lifted the tin hat off his head. The whole top of his head went with it. My mind just blanked. I was crouching there next to him, looking at the hole that was the top of his head. And his name, whoever he was, went out of my mind. There was nothing I could do. I didn't dare to put out my hand and touch him because I was so damned terrified. I was just crouching down in the ditch next to this dead man.

'That was when I first met the padre, Richard. He just appeared out of the smoke, dressed the same as I was, but with a dog collar and no gun. He knelt down to pray over the dead man with no top to his head.'

Sweat is running down over Harry's face, wetting his collar. It is spreading in damp stains under the single armpit of his shirt.

I insist that he moves off the wall and under the old pear tree, where it is cooler. I go into the yard to get some water. The gardener is there, with a hose attached to the brass tap, filling up a trailer full of watering cans. He goes into his building and wordlessly comes out with the old cracked mug, which I fill from the standpipe.

I go back and put the mug of water into Harry's hand.

Harry is turning to me, with terror in his eyes. I light the next cigarette for him. I ignite the match and transfer it to the tip of the cigarette. I become the flame that will take the heat off Harry's mind.

24

'We were exhausted. We'd had about an hour of sleep in two days. When you feel like that, you just go along from moment to moment doing whatever you are told. You rely on following orders.' Pausing, he takes a breath, then continues. 'So my memories of those days are a bit disjointed. I remember knowing that people were dying all around us. We'd come across civilians sitting dazed among the rubble of their homes. Towns where you didn't know what was what any more. Where the post office once stood, or the railway station...'

I pause, smoking my second cigarette. I can see what he is describing as vividly as blood. The terrible pictures that are engraved upon Harry's mind.

'I can see them now,' he murmurs softly, 'the columns of people walking. People wearing their best black coats, carrying a child in one arm and a bulging suitcase in the other. Or pushing something, anything that would roll. The lucky ones had donkeys and carts but they made use of anything – prams, wheelbarrows, carts with makeshift wheels, bicycles with bags strung over them.

'We were following on behind one of the armoured brigades. But they kept missing out pockets of the enemy, leaving us to deal with them.

'You find yourself shooting. There is no time for a careful aim. You shoot out the entire clip of your rifle.

It is a shock – a thrill, I am ashamed to say – when you know you have killed your first man.

'Passing through villages and towns without a sign of the enemy and then, suddenly, you encounter terrific resistance. We were fighting our way through barricaded streets with buildings on fire, and still we encountered fanatical resistance on every floor. "They're crazy!" Froggy would say. "They're out of their minds – when they know we're going to win this war!" You see, it made us angry the way they fought us all the way down to the cellars. They fought like hell and our friends died. Crossing the little roads and lanes between the ditches. We hated it every time we had to cross a lane.

'Maybe it would have been better if I'd been religious,' says Harry. 'So I could have fallen back on to the will of God. But for me it was just luck. A throw of the dice whether I survived or I didn't.'

Harry's face is shining, as mine must be shining. A common sweat is igniting our faces.

'On another occasion, my platoon was moving along the main street of some small town. Even to each other, we looked like ghosts in the smoke. All the time there was the sound of firing. Mortars going off. A machine gun rattling. You didn't know who was firing, or who they were firing at. Everything was burning. You couldn't see more than twenty yards because of the smoke. We moved from window to window, from door to door, smashing them in with our rifle butts and throwing grenades into the buildings in case of snipers.

'Day after day, more buildings burning. There could be civilians hiding in there. There was no way you could know, or allow for it.'

He talks on and on, in that same hushed voice. He describes a woman who appears out of a doorway. With a trembling hand, she holds out a photograph of her family, or her son or her husband. Sometimes a woman hands you a drink of water, or her last bottle of table wine. You give her cigarettes or chocolate in return. Sometimes she offers you sexual favours. And now and then you accept them, quick and furtive. And you pay back with the same. With chocolates or cigarettes.

'We'd come across Germans waving a white flag. We'd take their guns if we had the time, then pass them by. Leave them for somebody else to deal with. Once, we came across a group of local women beating a young German soldier to death with pieces of rubble. He had shot a girl who had run into him on her bicycle.

'I remember', says Harry, 'a small boy walking along the deep ruts left by the treads of a tank, with dirt on his face and his hands held high in the air.'

'It's terrible', he says, 'when one of your own is seriously wounded, moaning. Suddenly you are aware of the sound of a heavy machine gun firing. You try to determine where it is coming from. Within seconds it is a pitched battle, fought out over this street of rubble. Within minutes, the entire upper story of terraced buildings has flames coming out of the windows.

'Afterwards... the platoon sergeant, who had to take over from the dead lieutenant, told us to help the Padre with burial duties. Along the way, they had already made me up to corporal. Now I was acting sergeant, in charge of the burial detail. I recognised him from the beach, the Padre. Then we had to do the rounds, Froggy and me, searching through the ruins, to find the dead and the dying. We did our best. We'd put a leg or a head next to ...'

That inhalation again. The deep sigh, inwards, through the dilated nostrils.

'Sometimes you couldn't really say it was a man, or how many men, you were burying. It was just pieces of meat, bits and pieces, pieces of people.'

I am beginning to see the Padre now. I am beginning to see Richard Giles. Twenty-five years old. Brown hair swept back, caked in dust and sweat. The parting, I am guessing, on the left.

'He asked me for a cigarette.' In the still moment, as Harry pauses, I glimpse the Padre turning. The look in his eyes as, after he has prayed over the grave of a particularly gruesome mess, he asks acting Sergeant Harry Severn for a cigarette. Harry adds, 'I had never seen him smoke before.

'Anyway, I passed him the cigarette. I watched the Padre take his first puff of a cigarette.

'I asked myself, at that moment, why a padre would join us on the front line? You assumed that the chaplains stayed back, working in the field hospitals.'

'Froggy didn't know anything about it until the bomb went off. The booby trap they left there, just inside the door.'

We have arrived at another building in another burning town. Harry has no idea at all where he is, no idea of the name of the town that is burning down around him. The town where his friend, Froggy, has died. 'I remember', he says, 'the roaring of the flames, the rumble of falling masonry. An old woman in a black shawl looking at a pile of rubble, with shock in her eyes. We had shelled the church, because it was the most likely place where snipers would be waiting. It was one of their favourite places, waiting for us, in the windows of the steeple.'

Harry's own eyes are opened wide, remembering the old woman, who was holding a thin walking stick and searching for her spectacles, so she could look up at the ruins of her church.

'I went back to look for him, when the booby trap killed Froggy. I went back to find the Padre along the streets of the burning town. I found him kneeling in the shadow of one of the walls, ministering to a dying man. I came up to him and said nothing, waiting until he was finished.

'So we prayed over the dead, only this time it was Froggy we were praying over. I was looking down at Froggy's drawers, the "drawers cellular". Looking down... at the shreds of his drawers... sticking to his guts, as they were spilling out of him.

'I was sick. I felt this wave of giddiness and then I was sick next to Froggy, in the doorway.

'That was when he told me his name, Richard. After he wrote down the details in a little notebook he kept in his knapsack, so he could write back home to tell Froggy's mother and father that he had been with him. That he had prayed for him.

'That impressed me deeply. It impressed me that Richard was there with us, on the front line, so he could take down the details of their names so he could write a letter of comfort to every family.

'We buried Froggy in the first soft piece of ground we could find. Richard rolled up his sleeves and took a shovel in his own hands. He dug the shallow grave to bury Froggy, because I was too shocked to do it. He marked the grave so it could be dug up again later. So Froggy could be put into one of the proper war graves.'

I am shocked to find myself trembling. I am trembling, as Harry is trembling.

'That was when Richard put his arm around my shoulder. When he gave me his book. He talked to me about the madness of it all. And about his own feelings. It was unusual – with his being an officer, a Captain. He pressed the book into my hands and he told me that it was a special kind of book. He told me that the book contained some of the answers to the madness.'

I know the Padre better now. I can hear his voice, a calm voice, gently spoken – with an educated accent. Harry has told me that he was a Rhodes scholar. That he had come over from Salisbury, Rhodesia, and taken a philosophy degree at Oxford. This man, who was only five years older than Harry, who had moved from philosophy to enter the church.

Even in the dappled shade, Harry is still sweating. I don't think I have ever seen a man sweat so much without heavy physical work.

'It was something he once said to me, Froggy. I think it was the very first day we met, by our bunks in Richmond. "Me mam used to say to me that no matter what I did I'd be welcomed into heaven, because of the bass voice. But eternity is a long time singing for your supper, Harry. Do you think they'd make an exception for me? Let me shag a soprano now and then?"'

Harry's face, struggling to smile again at Froggy's joke.

'It was about a week later that we ran into the tanks. It was at a village called Cristot, somewhere close to the city of Caen. We were approaching the village through a cornfield. We didn't even know they were there. We had been told the place was undefended, a gap in their defences. But the 12th SS Panzers had moved in during the night. They were hiding behind the apple trees in a farm orchard.

'We had the support of nine Sherman tanks of the Dragoon Guards, but they didn't spot the Panzers. They went on ahead, through the orchard. In a few minutes seven out of the nine Shermans were burning. Taken from behind before they could even turn around.'

The sweat is altering the reflections on Harry's face, green seas of glistening points of sweat, like sunlight on a finely choppy sea.

'There's a term we used – brewing up. When a tank was hit, we'd say it was brewing up. When a tank caught fire.

'It was incredible, all that armoured metal, and yet they caught fire like that. They burned until the tops became red hot. We moved forwards into the orchard full of our burning tanks. One of them was going round and round in circles through the apple trees.

'One of our two battalion commanders was killed during the advance through the cornfield. The surviving commander took control of the two companies, and he ordered ours to move up on the right. We were to outflank the Panzers. My platoon was sent up along a sunken lane, edged with trees. That was where we ran into the tank. It came out of nowhere –

just suddenly appeared from behind a bend on a small slope. It was one of the smallest and oldest of the German tanks: a Panzer Mark IV. It opened fire with its machine gun, killing about half a dozen of us in the first few seconds.

'We dived into the gullies on either side of the lane. We took cover behind the trees, dodging backwards, trying to make our way to the company-held ground.

'Most of the platoon went off to the left, on the opposite side of the lane to me. The tank kept on coming. It was clanking down the lane, ripping up the gully on the other side from me with its heavy machine gun. Shooting what was left of us down like dogs. I could hear the screams as it was wiping them out one by one.'

I gaze upon a face that is trying to break through the terror. A face layered with different patterns and textures of sweat, like a ghost, with anxious eyes.

'Are you all right, Harry?'

He does not see or hear me.

'I saw Richard climb to his feet. I saw him stand up, come out from behind the trees across the lane. He was stumbling a bit, injured or wounded already. He had a white handkerchief in his hand and he was waving it from side to side. To end it now. To end the killing while there were still a few of us left.

'The tank was exactly opposite me, ignoring my side of the lane. I saw how the turret was starting to turn on its own, the whole tank following. The big wheel at the far side was stopped while the track on my side was churning up dirt. It turned surprisingly quickly. I saw it direct its machine gun on to the figure waving the white handkerchief. But he didn't take cover. I watched as it shot him to pieces.'

Harry's right cheek has become a mirrored glass, or a lake in half-shadow, green, or a hard semi-opaque jade of green.

'You see, a machine gun at twenty feet will literally do that. It will take you apart. Your head and body will just explode into a splatter of blood and flesh and bone.'

Harry's bald head has become a sea of reflections, pinpoints of light caught in a beam that falls through a gap in the leaves.

'I didn't understand any more. I didn't know what I was doing. When they did that. When they killed the Padre. It was as if it all... as if everything... everything that was bad in the world was right there, facing me... in that tank in the middle of the lane.'

It is as if his sweat has become one with his soul, with its need at last to come out into the open, to breathe in the sun.

'You see... I think, now... I know ... that I lost control.'

'Hey!' My voice is husky. Coughing to clear my throat, I am moving over, to put my arm around Harry's shoulders. But he will not accept it. He is shaking his head, forcing me away.

'The next thing I was aware of, I was standing up on to my shaky legs. I was hammering against the side of the tank with the butt of my rifle. I could see the SS sign, the two flashes of lightning, and the Eagle, the number and black cross on the side of the turret. I could see where the number was pushed up, where it went over a bulge in the armour. It was a battered old tank, blackened with fire and patched up from previous battles, a veteran from the Eastern Front.' Harry paused, a moment's reflection. 'Looking back – seeing it again in my mind – I know that inside the tank they were just men, like you and me. I couldn't even imagine what they had gone through. But I have to grant it to them, they know how to fight.

'I was ahead of it now. Having to stagger backwards, to stay in front of it because it had started once more to roll down the lane. I was shouting. Cursing and swearing. But they took no notice of me. The tank just kept rolling, bullets ripping through the gully and trees to my left.

'I couldn't hear my own voice because of the noise of the machine gun. I was shaking my fist at it. Choking on the stink. The main gun was level with my face.

'I must have emptied my rifle at it, for all the good that did me. If they even noticed me, the troops in the tank must have been laughing. Laughing at this mad Tommy. I suppose they thought they would run me over. All I had left was two hand grenades. I must have bitten off the pins without even thinking about it.'

I feel my own hand reach out. My hand is out, hurling the grenades under the tank, my head turning...

'I never saw what happened. Knocked out by the blast of my own grenades. I woke up back in field hospital.

'There was an officer from HQ who came to see me there and he told me what had happened. He said that two hundred and seventy officers and men died that day. They died in the cornfield and in the orchard. He wrote down the numbers for me because at first I was deaf. They included two-thirds of my platoon. He never mentioned the Padre, not specifically. Another thing he never mentioned was the opinion of the battalion commander, who got an MC for bravery. I didn't find that out until many years later. The commander felt very bitter about the outcome. He had opposed the attack, when the order had first come through. There was a term for it - a little piece of shorthand they used amongst themselves, the commanders in the field. An operation that wasn't "on". In his opinion, our battalion commander, the attack on Cristot had never been "on".'

Harry is blinking slowly, staring up over his head into the scanty leaves on the old pear tree. I light the match for him. I watch him draw on the cigarette.

'This officer who came to see me, he drew a sketch to show me how one of the grenades must have gone under a track. The explosion snapped the left track of the tank. Driving on just one track, it turned itself around and the big gun jammed between the trees. Made it a sitting duck for Corporal Burke, who put an anti-tank round into its side.'

I watch the mask of Harry's face as he struggles to find his thoughts again, as he struggles to surface, so that he can continue talking.

I listen to the quiet murmur of his voice explaining how he slowly recovered. How the grenade explosions had injured the nerves under his own right arm – because his right hand was still extended, in the act of throwing. There never was any shingles. I am hearing the real explanation for the pain that made Harry cut holes out of the right armpit of his shirts for more than fifty years.

'It was the battalion commander who recommended me for officer training. What I had done, the madness – he had written something silly, about an example or something.' A juddering pause, a lift of the head. 'They took me back and trained me.

'After the war,' he says, 'I stayed on in the army for a while. They were good to me. I rose to the rank of Major. Then, after I left the army, I joined the police at equivalent officer grade. I was appointed a Superintendent. A newly formed force they called the BSA. Not the bicycles - the British-South African police. I joined up with them because I wanted to go to Rhodesia. I wanted to go and meet Richard's parents. I had to go there and tell them face to face. I had to tell them about him, about his courage, about my admiration for what he had done.'

So that was how Harry had met Muriel, in Rhodesia. And that was where he also met Elizabeth, the young woman he would soon marry.

It was the early fifties. The world was coming out of darkness.

'People', he said, 'wanted to live again. They just wanted to enjoy themselves. They were hungry for it – they were hungry for happiness.'

25

I know now that my friend Harry is losing the battle. I sense this deep down in the marrow of my bones. The conversation about the war didn't do the trick; it just didn't work out the way I had hoped it would. And if ever there was a time when I desperately needed to think, this is the time. The trouble is, I don't know what I can do to help him. I'm feeling tired myself. So tired, I even considered catching the train at St Pancras station and heading back home to see Mum in Sheffield, just for a day or two, to try to clear my mind. But I couldn't make myself do it. Instead, I took it into my head that I would go and visit Muriel.

On the train to Cockfosters, there was a glare of sunshine coming in through the windows. I felt giddy throughout the journey. My heart was pounding and I couldn't get enough air into my lungs to breathe. I could have taken a taxi from the station but I needed the mile-long walk, past a golf course, to help clear my mind.

Before setting out I had gone back to The Palace and cleaned myself up. I had eaten some lunch and drunk two strong mugs of coffee, but I still felt anxious. Now I stood for what could have been minutes outside the gate of the small bungalow, giving myself a final chance of turning back. I didn't know if she would even be in. And maybe, in the state I was in, I might have hoped that she wasn't.

A ginger tom cat watched me as I rang the bell about half a dozen times. Then a woman's voice called out, 'Round the back!'

Muriel was sitting on a padded bench seat, in a wooden summerhouse in the back garden. Somebody had made an effort to hack back the lawn but the flowerbeds and bushes had a neglected look. I had to stand in the garden to talk to her - a thin woman wearing a flowery dress with short sleeves.

I had to guess that if she stood up, she would be about five feet five tall, as tall as Harry when she was wearing high heels. Her nose was beak-like and her eyes were slightly bulging, a darker blue than Harry's. Her chin was receding and her hair was short and white.

I told her who I was. Apologised for arriving on her doorstep without any prior introduction.

'I've been through all this several times with the social worker,' she said, warning me in advance that she was not going to change her mind.

There was a glass on the plank floor of the summerhouse, next to the blue sandal on her right foot. A long narrow glass, with a piece of lemon floating on an inch of clear liquid. I could easily smell the gin.

'Yeah, I know that, Mrs Severn.' I played the game of not knowing they weren't officially married. 'I can't even pretend it's an official visit. I've come here because of Harry. He's very upset.'

The dazzle of sunlight was still there in my eyes. The pounding heartbeat. The giddiness in my head.

'I'm really worried about him,' I added.

'I bet you are!' she murmured.

Her hand shook slightly as she reached down and picked up her glass, taking a sip and gazing past me into the garden. Her whole body was trembling slightly under the loose-fitting dress. There were two kinds of pills on a saucer: one pink and one large and white. She had got into the habit of carrying her pills around with her, to remind herself to take them.

'It's an awful thing – an awful thing to talk about, I know,' I said. 'But he has told me that he wants to die.'

She threw her head back and sniffed the air, as if she were sniffing some scent I couldn't smell. I wondered if she was sniffing at the honeysuckle that climbed over a wooden trellis on the path nearby.

'I suppose you know what he did? That he tried to strangle me?'

'Yeah. I'm really sorry, Mrs Severn.'

I found it hard to imagine Harry putting his hands around the thin, wrinkled neck of this old woman with the white hair. I thought that if he really had tried - the mind-blown Harry who had fought the six people when he first came in - that Muriel wouldn't be talking to me now.

There was a musty smell about her that seemed familiar. And something about her face – a hamster pouchiness to the angles of her jaw. Then I realised what it was. Her thinness was more than just a thinness. The muscles in her arms were wasted, like some of the people who came in and out of Turner Ward. It was the effect of alcohol on the nerves. If I reached out to touch that arm, the skin would feel hot and dry, sort of spongy to the touch. I found myself talking a bit loudly to cover up the fact that I had noticed this. 'He asked me to help him. That was what he said to me, Mrs Severn. He said, "Help me to die."'

She turned away from me again to look out somewhere else in the garden. It was a narrow garden, but quite long. The summerhouse had an angle to it. It had the shape of a thick wedge of cake. I wondered if there was a way of making it turn. If there was a lever somewhere that you could wind and the whole contraption with its old padded bench seat could be brought around to face the sun.

"'Help me to die!'" she repeated my words.

So I was beginning to wonder if she had the brain rot that went with the damaged nerves.

Then she spoke to me in this clipped voice and she didn't sound foolish at all. It was a taut kind of a voice, to be honest with you, because of the anger that was there under the quaveriness that was caused by her shaking. 'I can see that he has made a fool of you, the way he makes a fool of everybody,' she said.

She finished off her glass and poured another couple of inches of neat gin out of a bottle I hadn't noticed, behind her legs.

'If it is any consolation to you,' she said, 'he made a fool out of me too.'

Her voice had a slight accent to it. A Rhodesian accent.

She refused my help when she groaned with the effort of climbing up, pushing herself out of the summerhouse with the help of a walking stick and hobbling before me on the tarmac path, heading for the back door.

At the door she turned and said, 'You'd better come on into the house.'

The place smelled rankly of cat. The furniture was of dark oak. A Welsh dresser had those cups and saucers you never used, covered in the Willow pattern. There were African things on the wall and on the sideboard. Masks and elephants carved out of dark brown wood. And photographs. When you had a proper look round, it was the photographs that really hit you. It was the photographs she had brought me in to see. Muriel was the photographer and it was the one thing she was really proud about. She leaned for support against the table while I took the guided tour.

I was interested anyway.

There were some African huts in scorched yellow grass. Wild places, where beasts with strange horns stuck their heads out of the shadows. A baby monkey hanging on to its mother next to a river. Behind the river were chalk-blue mountains. There were bushes that looked as if they had sprung into fire. She told me the bushes were called poinsettias. It took me a few seconds with one of the pictures to make out the green and yellow chameleons on the surface of silvery grey rocks. A hammer kop bird perched over a pool. An African crow, with a white ring around its neck, was pecking at the ground.

'Is this you?' I asked her.

'That's me,' the clipped voice replied.

'You're beautiful. You only look eighteen.'

"K'you!' she said. That same clipped tone as Freda's daughter. The thank you that didn't really mean it.

The younger Muriel looked handsome rather than beautiful, the way all those anorexic models look. Her hair was the colour of sun-bleached straw. Muriel was posing for the camera, crouching down to admire a flower with a head like a full dandelion clock, only brilliant crimson.

I said to her, 'So this picture must have been taken by Harry.'

She didn't answer. But you could see why Harry fancied her, with her sun-tanned arms and legs, her short-cropped blonde hair, the small fine beak of a nose.

'The photographs are really beautiful.'

She jerked her head away.

'Come and look at these!' she declared proudly, beating at the floor with her stick as she took me through to another room.

I could see that she liked waterfalls.

She had blown them up. Huge colour photographs about two feet square. Dreamy pictures of waterfalls, as good as anything I have ever seen. Trees were rising up out of swirling mists that were blotting out the blue of the sky.

Then she recharged her glass from a litre bottle that stood on the sideboard and she took the glass with her, just about falling into one of the armchairs, covered in a sun-bleached chintzy cover.

It felt really strange, sitting down face to face with Harry's Muriel. I thought about the fact that she was a lot younger than Harry, probably no more than in her mid sixties.

She said, 'I was a farmer's daughter. We hardly saw a new face in months, and then Harry arrived. I heard about him even before I ever met him: the war hero. I first saw him at a dance in the church hall. I just stared at him, at the erectness of him, the way he stood. There was a toned, manly look about him. Full of confidence. As if life was his for the taking. And when he danced with you, you felt your feet were lifted off the ground.'

'How do you mean, war hero?' I asked her.

'You know they gave him a medal?'

I shook my head.

'Why, that was why he came out in the first place! He felt he didn't deserve it. He wanted to give it to Richard's family in Salisbury. His Military Medal.'

I was staring into her eyes, astonished that Harry hadn't mentioned this.

'It's over there, if you want to look at it,' she added abruptly, bitterly. 'In that drawer, to the left.'

My legs were slightly shaky as I stood up and opened the drawer. I had to rummage around for the medal, which was in a brown leather presentation case.

I could hear her talking in the room behind me. She said, 'It was a ridiculously sentimental thing to do. Of course they wouldn't take his medal.'

The medal was silver-coloured, about an inch across, on the end of a blue ribbon with three white vertical stripes. There was a picture of King George on the front and on the back was Harry's name, *Sgt H. E. Severn, For Bravery in the Field.*

'Too mean to give him the cross. If he had truly been commissioned in the field – if he really were an officer, then', she called out, 'it should have been the cross. It's different now – but back then they didn't give crosses to ordinary soldiers. Only to the officers.'

I put the medal back into its drawer, then pushed the drawer shut.

I could see that my presence was upsetting her, because she had crossed the floor to help herself to another two inches of gin.

I said to her, 'I can see it in the photographs. How happy you must have been.'

She had a way of looking at you, Muriel. A quick movement in her neck, the way a bird moves. A kind of a hawk's profile, I would say.

'The waterfall pictures – they're really great. I think they're the most beautiful pictures I've ever seen.'

She actually flushed then. This emaciated old lady, canned on gin.

I spoke to her gently, urgently: 'Why won't you go and see him? He's really upset about things. About what he did.'

'You think I'm a bitch because I won't go and see him?'

I suppose she knew she embarrassed me then, because her eyes fell, then lifted up again to look into mine. I suppose she knew she was saying too much, because there was a look in her eyes that I recognised. I had felt it often enough myself, after Tabi.

'No, I don't think that at all.' I hesitated, dropped my own eyes from contact with her eyes.

'We'd get drunk', she said, proudly, quietly, 'on expensive champagne. 'Me – Muriel Livesey, the Methodist farmer's daughter. Champagne in the morning. Champagne for breakfast. He blew away all of the lump sum he was given by the army. He had no intention of waiting for the sun to set.' She lifted that hawk's beak to sniff at the air again. 'How can I explain to you ... that there was such a feeling about him. Such energy - such a devil-may-care! He was different to anybody I had ever met. It was as if - as if he had been chosen, so nothing could trouble him.'

'Yeah!' I muttered. 'Chosen by a toss of the blood-stained dice!'

But she wasn't listening to me. Her nose was sniffing at the air in the room. Her eyes were distant, glowing.

'It was wonderful. He taught me how to do the cha-cha-cha. And we'd do it, wild in the bush. I was eighteen years old, dancing under the stars.'

Muriel recharged her glass with neat gin. She must have gone through about a quarter of the bottle in the short time I was with her.

'What did you say your name was?'
'Mylie.'
'Mylie!' she laughed then. 'Well, Mylie,' she interrupted my ruminations, 'I don't suppose you have ever been to Rhodesia?'
'No, I haven't.'
'Oh, I wish you had been to Rhodesia. Then you'd know what I am talking about. Not only are you close to the tropics, but you are also very high. The sky - that wonderful night sky is incredible. The Milky Way burns

right through the sky, it dominates the heavens – like a river made up of millions of souls. In the morning, we'd watch the sun come up into a perfect blue.

'I used to wake at dawn just to see that, even when I was a girl, growing up in our beautiful house. There was a tree in the garden, full of lilac blossom. A jacaranda tree as tall as the house.

'We'd go for walks. I'd take him to my secret places, the places I had found on my own as a girl. That was the exciting part - growing up near to baboons and leopards. You would hear the troop of baboons barking – *qwaqwaqwa-qwa!* They'd come up and bark at you and then run away.' Muriel hesitating again. The faraway look in her eyes.

'There was a little crevasse. I told Harry about it. I showed him the place where the leopards would hide in the heat of the day.' There was a change in her voice. A note of joy, of longing.

'Can you believe the madness of the man? The reason I fell head over heels in love with him?' Her voice was like a high-pitched cry, like a baby's cry, rising out of the force of her memories.

'You see, we would lie out there, together, in each others arms, night after night. In the lairs of leopards. We could hear them coughing nearby, waiting for us to go at dawn, as still we lay in each other's arms.'

'So, what went wrong?'

'Elizabeth. Oh, Elizabeth was a thing even then. She would never allow anything to be mine, not even when we were children. My cousin Elizabeth. And I knew she would win, once she put her mind to it. She was four years older and a lot better at it than I was. I could see that, once they got together. There was no longer any room for me.'

'So Harry married Elizabeth, your cousin.'

'Harry married Elizabeth.' Her eyes were still lost in the past, her arms folded about herself in the lairs of leopards.

'But he came back to you?'

'Twenty-seven years ago. When Elizabeth left him. When he wouldn't go with her to Australia. She couldn't take the climate here.'

'They had a son, Teddy?'

'Yes. Elizabeth and Teddy.'

'Why didn't he go to Australia with her?'

She had to pause, to think. Thinking about more than just my question. She said, 'I think it was the job, you know. That and the beginning of common sense.'

'What job?'

'He had gone to night classes, after trying all sorts of things. Oh, he was always very enterprising, Harry. But every one of his enterprises failed. He even tried setting up dances. Old fashioned ballroom dancing in big hotels – that sort of thing.'

'The dancing didn't work out?'

'The new music had arrived. The rock'n'roll.'

'What did he study, at the night classes?'

'Work study engineering. He really took to it, because it meant working with people. Mainly with factories that were in the clothing trade. He was good at it. Loved it. Loved the people. He used to say that he was the only one in the factory who knew everybody, who knew what they coveted from life. He took a pride in knowing what everybody was really thinking. I don't think there was a single factory he ever went into where he didn't improve the efficiency. That was why he didn't go with Elizabeth. He was annoyed with her because she wouldn't wait for him and he had just got a big job, one that would keep him for a year.'

'So she went without him.'

Ignoring me, she said, 'I went with him to have drinks with one of the managing directors. It was in his office - a Polish man whose name I cannot recall. He was amazed that Harry had gone into his factory and improved efficiency by thirty per cent. I can remember the way he turned around, after he had taken the brandy back to the cabinet behind us. He just stood there and suddenly declared, "I know what it is, Harry! I have solved it! It's because you have an honest face."'

'He wrote to you then? When Elizabeth left?'

'Harry never wrote. He telephoned. I had just got back with my father from the cattle market. The message was there. To call Harry.' Muriel was nodding her head. Smiling, a wistful little smile. 'After eighteen years. I was thirty-six years old and still unmarried, but Harry had remembered me. He was coming back for me. I was getting him back from Elizabeth, just as eighteen years earlier she had taken him from me. It was me he had wanted all along.'

We went back out into the garden because she wanted to sit in the summerhouse again. She showed me how it turned all right, demonstrating how to move it around. I had to push the whole thing physically so she could sit there on the padded seat and feel the sun directly on her face. Then she poured me a glass of tonic water and she cut me a slice of lemon to float in it.

'But I don't understand. Why?'

'Why?' Shaking her head with bitterness – a terrible, deeply-felt bitterness. 'Perhaps I never really understood him. A few years ago, he became obsessed with seeing Teddy again. With making it up to him.'

'And Teddy didn't want to know?'

She snorted. 'I watched his face - Harry's face. Do you know what Teddy said to him?'

I shook my head, sipping the tonic water. Watching the ginger tom crouch at the bottom of a tree, in which there was a family of squirrels.

'After all those years, he called them up in Australia. And do you know what Teddy said to his loving father? "Why don't you go drop dead, Dad."'

She looked at me now, this woman, who had been wounded so badly it showed in her eyes.

'I was glad,' she said. 'It's no good pretending otherwise. Because he was doing it again. Elizabeth had won.'

I said, 'Oh Harry – you bloody lunatic!'

'I know it is a terrible thing to say,' she said to me, 'but I don't care any more about Harry. I don't care because of what he did to me,' she murmured. 'After twenty-seven years.'

I arrive home to a house that is cloaked in silence, wallowing in darkness. They have found somewhere else to carry on with the celebrations. I am glad. I am relieved about that, to be honest with you. I feel so wound up, I take two cans of beer from the fridge and go up to my room.

I am consumed by restlessness.

I know the feeling now. I know just where I am. I am down there, now, Harry. I am down there with you, at the bottom of your well. And the feeling is so awful. It is such a terrible feeling.

I love the music but I haven't actually heard it for more than a year. After I have put the CD in the deck, I automatically switch out the light. I lie motionless on my bed and listen to the greatest blues recording ever made by a white voice: Uliet Van Vliet, alias Captain Beefheart, the 'Tarot Plane' track on the *Mirror Man* compilation. *Christ – oh, Jesus!* I am clinging on here to his growling harmonica voice.

If you are musical and you have never heard Captain Beefheart in your life before, it hits your senses something like a tsunami. But tonight, for me, it is cooling, wonderfully soothing.

I wonder at people and what they do. I wonder at what people do to each other. My bewilderment goes round and round in my head, as I can hear Captain Beefheart singing it now, in that gruff bluesy voice, *'You gonna need somebody awn yo' mind'*. The growly harmonica rolling and whorling.

I have to give up wondering, knowing you can't understand a quarter of what it is that people will do to each other in this crazy world.

I lie still, moving only through my breathing, through the hoarse vibrations in my throat and my chest. The only illumination in the room is the digital array on the deck. And still the feelings rise up out of me. The feelings just rain out of my heart and there is no stopping them. I am still struggling, searching for explanations, finding the need to explain, as if life itself depended on this understanding.

I think that maybe Van Vliet, in some of his great tracks such as 'Electricity' and 'Autumn's Child', was feeling his way right down there to the abstract soul of serious music, the place where you find the Mozarts and Mahlers, the kind of people who take the risk of being misunderstood. And, make no mistake about it, that's where they are heading. This is what Beefheart discovered for himself. People don't like it when you take those risks. They strip the flesh off your bones. You have to take the pain of that. You have to let them strip the flesh off your bones and then they set fire to what is left.

You've got to think what is left. What is left, when you are watching your bones go up in flames. All that is left is your soul. It's the only thing they can't get to.

That's the way you have to find your way through. That it is the only thing that is absolutely yours, absolutely untouchable.

Right now, I am burning up in myself. I have to pause to take a rest in my mind. Maybe I don't want to understand anymore. I don't think I can face just what it is I am feeling. If I could weep, I would be weeping now. Only I stopped weeping a long time ago, sitting in the car next to my mother when I was eight years old.

26

I am going to have to take care of Harry. I know the seriousness of it. You don't decide on such a course of action without a great deal of thought. I have been changing my mind a hundred times a day, but I keep coming back to it. Because I know now that Muriel will not come to see Harry, and Harry will die. Harry is going to die because Muriel cannot forgive him. Because Muriel, for entirely understandable reasons, has run out of forgiveness.

So that is what I am thinking now, thinking so much my mind is out of gear from the stress of it, my body tired out from the lack of sleep.

And from realising that there is no choice. No choice at all.

Today, all day, I have been struggling to come to terms with this while specialing a new admission. I have had to special this patient because nobody else was willing to do it. Everybody is terrified of him. They are all demanding - all of the nurses are demanding - that he should be taken out of the Unit and put into a secure place. A place where they have the facilities to take care of people who frighten other people.

Even Maggie was a little frightened of him when she came to write down his history. I saw the fear in her eyes as she began, 'Hi, Ruel!'

Sitting on the two mattresses, he was as tall as Maggie standing up. The tension of his outrage was bending Ruel's body over, his back curving down, his neck following the sweep of his back, cradling the symbol of it all, hugging its small, squat shape.

Maggie had not yet managed to press the right button. That was the reason why he had nothing to say. I was glad I was there looking after Maggie, who was terrified out of her wits, her eyes darting over, her eyes making sure I was there from moment to moment throughout the interview.

'Will you tell me how old you are, Ruel?'

Ruel does not answer.

'Will you tell me your date of birth?'

Still Ruel does not reply.

Maggie is leaving us next week. There will be no more watching those small hands shaking with determination as she gives a patient the ECT. No more helpful conversations in the kitchen.

'What do you think has gone wrong with your life? Why do you think you have been brought into hospital?'

You can't blame Maggie, whose job it is to ask such questions. It isn't her fault that they are irrelevant to Ruel in this desperately charged situation. And Ruel tries. You can see how hard he is trying because there is a pause now and then - a thinking pause. Maggie senses this too and so, patiently, she starts all over again:

'Was it something that upset you – something that happened when you went in to school?'

Ruel doesn't answer her questions because he doesn't know how to answer her questions. Because scared as Maggie is of him, he is far more scared of her. Ruel is feeling so terrified that his mind cannot come to terms with ordinary things. His mind cannot recognise these ordinary things because, all of a sudden, the world feels wrong to him. There is nothing he recognises in the world any more.

Ruel is suffering from acute paranoid schizophrenia. It began today. Yesterday he was a normal kid, studying for his A-levels at school. Today he finds himself in an alien world – a world where, according to the voices in his head, everybody he meets is plotting against him.

I had arrived at my usual late shift time of 1.45 and there was history repeating itself. This enormous black lad was lying on the carpet in front of Reception, with people struggling to hold him down. Not six people this time. This time we weren't dealing with awkward Harry. The four policemen who brought Ruel in were helping Alan, and about ten more of the staff - nurses, doctors, one administrator and now one additional HCA – and we were all struggling like hell to restrain him without injuring him. We had to throw a mattress over him so we could give him a sedative injection. This was a new one to me, the mattress trick. But even with the mattress he was so big his head was out of one end and his feet were poking out of the other end. I had shared a sudden panic with Maggie when the police had driven away from the entrance in their van, leaving us to take care of Ruel.

I found myself rising up out of my own desperation, thinking, Hey, Maggie – listen to me. Believe me. I can speak for him. I can answer for this lost and bewildered soul. Because, desperation for desperation, I know the way in.

I could have answered Maggie's questions. I could have told her that it doesn't matter, who he is or what has brought him in. It doesn't matter to Ruel whether he knows or he doesn't know where he is. Whether this is a hospital or the secure unit – or San Quentin Prison in sunny California. This eighteen-year-old black youth, whose mind has gone supernova. Whose life is unlikely ever to return to normal. Whose new understanding dawned in an A-level class when he opened up his desk and began to hurl his books at his teacher and his fellow pupils.

So now I wait for Maggie to enter the diagnosis, to place Ruel into his box. We have made a little progress. The clue to Ruel is right here, clenched in his hand; it is in the music he is carrying, the CDs in the box he has wrapped himself around, every one of them by Jimi Hendrix.

I help Maggie out, nodding, with a smile. 'They always ask you your name, but they don't give you the code for the answer.'

A growl.

'They ask you all these questions. I mean, their own mothers wouldn't know the answers to some of those questions. You'd need the book to answer some of those questions.'

Ruel is chuckling.

So I hunch down a little closer to him. On the two mattresses in the room where you cannot kill yourself through the plugs or the lights. Where your laces have been taken from your oversize trainers. I sense the shudder of a frightened boy within his huge body. I sense the panic that crouches inside, like an embryo of terror.

'Hey!' I laugh. 'You have to grant it to Jimi – he did it the hard way. It took him a long time to get there, but he got there.'

He is nodding. No meeting of eyes, of course. I don't expect that. I have been here before.

'The interesting thing is that it was London where he made it.'

'Yeah!'

'And the way he died, old Jimi Hendrix. I just can't believe it, the way it happened. It was such a loss.' I catch the wondering glance from Maggie, but I mean every word of what I am saying. I too am a great admirer of Jimi Hendrix. 'If ever anybody deserved better, Jimi did. He deserved better than to go out like that, surrounded by a bunch of sycophants.'

Now Ruel is shaking his head. You would need to see him do this to witness the passion in this gesture. 'I didn't die, man. I cannot die. I never died.'

I am having trouble sleeping. I am struggling to bring myself to go to work. My heart is pounding and waves of gooseflesh crawl over my skin. I feel faint while doing the ordinary chores. It's all caused by the worry of what I know, the worry of what is happening to Harry. That, together with the lack of sleep. On one occasion, while doling out the laundry on Constable, I have to sit down and let Alice make me a cup of tea.

I mean, people do die on the ward. I remember when I first arrived we had two die in the same week, and everybody was a bit freaked out then too.

Mary is sneaking down the corridor, carrying a bulging bin-bag over her shoulder. As she passes by me on Turner Ward, she says, 'Excuse me, but could you tell me the way out of this place?'

I murmur, 'You know who it is, Mary. It's me – Mylie.'

'Oh, it's you, is it, Gorgeous?'

I glance at Ruel, who is currently resting. His eyes are closed, his body curled on to its side, so he can fit it on to the mattresses.

Mary comes up to me, where I am sitting on the chair in the doorway of the Safe Room, specialing Ruel. She whispers, 'I'm only going out into the corridor.'

'I see, Mary,' I whisper back. Working out what is in the bin-bag, which is two full sets of clothes.

'How is Lesley?'

'Oh, much better now, Mylie.'

I can tell from Mary's body language that it really is a good sign. It tells me that Lesley is doing okay. Just as Leslie assumes the personality of Mary, Mary is the mirror of Leslie's hurt.

'Her mind is clear?'

'Oh, absolutely! Oh, she understands.' Now Mary is peering furtively up and down the corridor. 'We have seen the Lord. We have seen the hand of the Lord in all things.'

This is a new avenue of communication between myself and Mary, this Lord business. But it is comforting. I sense that Mary is feeling comfortable with this, in the body language, the tone of her voice. Somebody is shouting out, 'Nurse! Nurse!' She whispers, with a cunning expression on her face, 'Oh, the baby will be beautiful. This is the promise of the Lord. We have felt the will of the Lord in all things now.'

I have no idea about this baby. Whose baby it is, or if it's imaginary or real, as I watch Mary sprinting towards the stairs.

There is a kind of antenna here on the Unit. A feeling for the impending storm, like a common vibration. We all have it. We all feel this pressure building up. We all experience this pitch of tension.

It is manifesting its disturbing presence through the background of romantic bust-ups. Anna has broken it off with Martin, a staff nurse on Turner, who is threatening suicide – or so the rumour machine has it. So Anna spends half the day putting her arm around him to break it off gently. Meanwhile she is into her wide-eyed look, her jokey-with-Mylie stage, her touchy-feely-with-Mylie stage. It is such a terrible irony that I am the focus of all this promising foreplay when it is too late.

'You've got to fight it,' I shout at Harry. 'Dammit, Harry – you can't just give in!'

My mind is so exhausted, I just can't think of anything clever to say. Any really clever argument to turn his mind around. I haven't told Harry about going to see Muriel. There just wouldn't be any point in telling him that.

Harry is just scratching at his head, making flakes of skin fall from the freckled scalp.

'Jesus, Harry!' I am rubbing at my eyes. I am almost dozing off myself, because I am so physically tired. So lacking in sleep.

But it's no good. There's nothing there, no response. If I could go in through his eyes I would find myself in a hollow place.

So I have to try this one last time. It's the reason why I have come up here to his room. I have to play it smarter somehow. I have to open up this terrible subject with Harry.

'We had a headmaster at school called Mr Jolly. That was his name, but he was anything but. One of the first things he told us all at assembly when we first arrived out of Junior School was, "Don't think you have come here so we can teach you to be clever." So all the bright kids would know just where they stood.'

I'm thinking: Mr Jolly wasn't looking at the likes of me. Not the nephews of taxi drivers.

'What was irritating Mr Jolly was the fact we came from a mixed area, so there were people like Tabi, who came from more wealthy parents. The kind of kids whose parents had expectations. I mean, we were all just eleven years old in that assembly hall, but we knew what he was saying. He was saying that this is a factory and we are going to grind you out.

'When I think of him now, I see that old guy in the film about the Czar of Russia and his family – the scrawny old gaoler with a skull for a face who got out of his chair when the order came to shoot them. He had that same tired look when he was reaching for his revolver.'

I hesitate, blinking. Waiting for him to argue back. I am trying to fight off the feeling I need to lie down.

'It is unlikely that Mr Jolly was a believer in the idea of genius. But one day something happened that made me think my headmaster was wrong.

'I must have been fifteen years old. And Miss Chalmers was our art teacher. She had mousy hair that was turning grey. We all took advantage of her because she was a gentle person who hated having to impose discipline. But you could see she really loved her work. One day she took the whole class to Chatsworth House, which is only about ten miles outside Sheffield. A lot of the kids were trying to get away, out into the grounds below the terrace, to smoke or generally mess around. But I stayed with the group she took through the big rooms. We got to a painting by Rembrandt. Miss Chalmers was standing there, just looking at the painting, which showed the face of an old man. She told us that Rembrandt was a genius. And the nature of his genius was the way he could weave into the faces he painted the knowledge that we are all dying from the moment we are born.

'It was probably the only time we listened attentively to her. I remember how we all looked really hard into the face in the picture.'

Now, studying Harry, watching him yawn, I understand a little more of what was going through the mind of Rembrandt. I know how you really can be dying a little at a time, from day to day.

27

Yeah, you have to think about it. And the days go by and you change your mind a hundred times, thinking about it. But you keep on coming back to it. You know you have to do it. You know there is no choice. No choice at all. You have to plan it clearly in your mind.

I said to him, to my friend, Harry,
 'My Uncle Tony is a bit of a character. If you met him, you'd really like him.' He was putting his right arm through the sleeve of the shirt, negotiating his way past the hole he had cut, and now I was fastening the cuff.
 'Everybody likes him, my Uncle Tony. I mean, every time you meet him, he has some new joke to tell you.' I had to hold the shirt low down behind him, so he could manoeuvre his left hand backwards into the sleeve. 'And I'm not talking about jokes off the television or maybe picked up from the Labour Club. I'm talking about jokes he thinks up by himself. Jokes to do with the weather that day, or something that has just happened in the family, or even the kind of trouble I am in with my mum, when I happen to be in trouble.'

He was looking up at me now, because I was doing so much talking. Our eyes met. I bit off this hangnail piece of my right thumb nail, which was sharp and catching.

I fastened the buttons down the front of his shirt. When Harry came in he could have done them for himself but now he had the retardation. I could feel the lead in his muscles when I was helping him move his arms.

'But there is one thing, one weakness, with Tony,' I added, helping him to tuck his shirt into the waistband of his hospital issue baggy grey trousers, 'and that's the fact he is self-conscious about his bald head.'

I managed the pullover. I got him into it without a fight. I was reaching out for the jacket – Harry's own pin-strike jacket, the one he was wearing when he came in – when Harry said, 'I don't want to wear the jacket.'

'I think it might be a good idea.'

'I don't care what you think. I'm not wearing the jacket.'

I stopped to look down into his obstinate eyes. It was the third week since he had completed the ECT.

'Okay, so you're not wearing the jacket.' I put the jacket, folded, back down on the bed. I went down on my haunches to make a start with the Oxford brogue shoes. 'So my mother, Brenda, and my Aunt Lizzie – Tony's wife, Lizzie – got together to buy Tony this wig. They went with him to help him pick it. And he wore it for his fortieth birthday when they went to Aintree, so he could go and see the Grand National, wearing his Johnny Cash rug.'

Harry was starting to chortle. Loosening up. It made it easier for me to slip the jacket on to his lap, when I got him sitting in the wheelchair.

I should have shaved him first but I forgot because I had other things on my mind. So I shaved him now, where he was sitting in the chair, with a towel around his neck. And then I trimmed his moustache. I made Harry look neat and tidy.

'Anyway,' I laughed – I couldn't help laughing, just thinking about Tony. 'He took to wearing the rug all the time. Even when it came to going out to work. He'd wear it with this serious look on his face, when he was driving around the place in his taxi. But then the other taxi drivers pulled his leg. Up to now it was Tony who was always sharp with the jokes. Now they were getting one over on him. They'd sing that old tune, you know – "Here we go again, happy as can be", only instead of "here", they'd sing "Hair we go again". They'd whistle it, just the opening line, but Tony would know it. You wouldn't believe how long he put up with it. But then, one day, he just couldn't take it any more and so he put the rug back into its box.'

Harry was just about ready. As a last thing, I put his bowler hat on his head. He looked great, he really did, if you weren't aware of the retardation.

'But the funny thing was,' I said, struggling a little to get him through the door. 'The funny thing,' I repeated myself, once we were in the first of the corridors, 'was when he put it away, it was as if a miracle was happening. My Uncle Tony came out again. He came out from under the rug like the sun coming out from behind a cloud. He was sharp again. He was sharper than ever, in first with the jokes.'

We were passing by the nurses' office. My heart was somewhere about the level of my throat. I needed to pick up Harry's medication from the cupboard.

I called to Alison, who was nearby. I asked her if she knew where Michael was. I already knew, of course. Michael was attending the big management meeting. He was airing our grievances about the late arrival of meals. I didn't have to pretend to be harassed. I was taking Harry for his daily rounds. And he was going to miss out his afternoon medication. Even then Alison was aware there was something wrong. There was something here that didn't add up but she wasn't sure enough to stop me. The key was out on the end of her chain, Harry's medication taken out of the cupboard. I shook out a single dose, enough for just one day. I would square it with Michael later, I told her. I reassured her with my beamingly honest smile as she was sliding the chain back into her pocket.

Still no Michael. My heart was still up there in my throat, beating.

We had to negotiate Jock, doing his thing. Nod to Donald, the artist, in his cords and string vest. I was whistling as I walked Harry towards the lift, listening to the swishing sound of the two big wheels on the carpet.

We didn't even have the lift to ourselves. John squeezed in, the Court Diversion Officer. John, of all people: the nurse who first brought Harry into the Unit. I just nodded a friendly hello to John, let him out first as we emerged into the downstairs corridor, out past Reception, smiling to Anna. Anna, who was staring after me, disappointed with my failure to connect, now that her focus had found my direction. Out then, through the first of the glass doors. We were through the second pair of doors.

We were outside now and the sun was shining, baking hot for the first week in June. That was the reason I had put the hat on his head. Old Harry, who was fretful already because of the jacket, which was still lying on his lap.

'I'll carry it', I said, 'as soon as we are in the taxi.'

It was the first time I mentioned the taxi. And I knew now what Harry was thinking. Thinking slowly, because his mind was slowing down too with the retardation, as we negotiated the flowerbeds, as we passed by the central circle of blooming roses. I could hear the diesel engine turning over, on the far side of the flower garden. But the awkward Harry wouldn't wait. We had to stop there next to the roses while I removed the jacket from his lap. I had to carry it folded over my arm.

'What's this about a taxi?'

'I'm taking you to Brighton, Harry. To where you used to walk Nobby on the beach.'

'Brighton my eye!'

He was resisting me, refusing even to climb out of the wheelchair now, with the driver looking on. I looked up into the sky with frustration. Casting a sly glance back to the two-storey building, I wouldn't have been at all surprised to see startled faces peering down at us out of the window.

'Come on, Harry.' I couldn't help worrying that Michael's face had appeared. Perhaps he was already picking up a phone or running down the stairs.

Harry declared, in his soldier's voice, 'You and your girl! You had it all. You had more than it all. Why did you break up?'

'For pity's sake, you've got to help me.'

The eyes were now confronting mine. The blue eyes, demanding barter. 'She left you, didn't she?'

'Yeah. That's right,' I urged him on, with my voice hoarse. 'You can read me like a book, Harry.'

The soldier's rasp. 'Because you were screwing around. Because you just couldn't stop yourself. You dirty little sod!'

Anxiety was screaming against the roof of my head.

'No.'

'Liar!'

'I had been there already. Done that. Realised the uselessness of it.'

'Liar!'

'Look, you can believe whatever you want to believe.' I had to fold the jacket over the cloth back of the chair, to free my hands to prise him out of it. From the corner of my eye, I saw the driver climbing out of his cab.

Harry was relishing the trouble he was putting us to, me and the driver. We had to lift him on to his feet.

I whispered it, like a whiplash, into his ear, 'All right, Harry. It was me. My fault.'

'I knew it.'

Going sort of limp now, which was just another of his tricks, as between us we hefted the limp Harry along the path, having to daddy him into the back of the taxi. I had to go back to the wheelchair to fetch his jacket.

'Will you tell me?' The implicit threat that otherwise he was going to cause trouble.

'Yeah, I'll tell you.'

Harry was sitting back now, slumped against the seat rest. The driver was still outside, examining the chair to see if it would fold up.

'Can't get it into the cab, mate!'

'It doesn't matter,' I said through the open door. 'Somebody will come out and pick it up.'

He was looking uncertain, shaking his head, so I made a display of getting out again and pushing the chair on to the grass. I very visibly applied the brake.

Back now, sitting beside him, I had to give Harry his due. I accepted his price for our tickets out.

'I got obsessive, Harry. I got carried away. Is that what you wanted to hear?' We were jerking and juddering around as the vehicle was moving off, towards the road that goes around the Unit and into the hospital grounds.

'You got jealous.'

'I got so I wanted to own every part of her.'

'She gave you reason for that? For jealousy? She was messing you around?'

'Not really. Just the usual little things. She'd smile when somebody said hello. An old boyfriend would send her a birthday card – or a Valentine.' I lied easily. I find that I can do that without the slightest compunction.

'It was the Valentine, am I right?'

'Maybe.'

To be honest with you, I just didn't care. I didn't care what it was. But I didn't want to make this too obvious. I didn't want to make it too easy for him.

'So tell me about it.'

In moments, it seemed, we were passing along the familiar route. We were turning right where I had to rush him that day, hauling the groaning Harry to the red brick lavatory. Already we had left it all behind. We were moving away from the Abandoned Garden. We coursed along the hundred yard stretch of the main hospital buildings, baking in the heat. A left through the main hospital gates, then a right on to the road outside. I glimpsed it then, for barely a moment: the disbelieving look on Harry's face. Harry, who was no longer a patient. Harry who had become a person once more. At the lights, the driver leaned across to open the window on the left side of his cab, the window on the right already open. The reason he did that was because Harry had extracted a cigarette, ignoring the no-smoking sign in the passenger compartment. Harry just didn't give a damn about the rules, lighting up as we were heading citywards now, for the radial artery that would become the Edgware Road.

I said, 'There was one particular boyfriend. That's all there was to it. It was the fact that he and Tabi ... they travelled a certain distance together.'

'She did it with him before she did it with you!'

I sighed, glancing towards the driver, who couldn't help but take an interest. I caught his eyes in the rear view mirror. Harry was bawling it all out in his officer's voice. I had the feeling that the whole world was listening to me.

'No.'

'But they must have been messing around. He was the first?'

'Jesus, Harry!'

'He was the first. And you knew she liked it.'

'She said it meant nothing.'

Harry smiling triumphantly.

Of course I hadn't believed her when she had said that. She had said that just to avoid hurting me, because of my jealousy.

I just said it now. Through gritted teeth. 'It was a thing they did that irritated me. They kissed each other all over.'

'How do you mean?'

'You heard what I said.'

'What – all over their bodies?'

I said nothing.

'That's women for you. Women!' Harry was laughing so much now. Laughing until there were tears in his slowly blinking eyes.

'So that was it? What drove you mad?'

'No,' I think back. 'No. It was me. Something in me. My response to the closeness of it, to the spiritual intimacy of what we had. Thinking I wanted to own every part of her. I wanted to own every living cell in her body. The entire surface of her skin.'

'Ah!' Harry was coming to life. He was getting round to enjoying this.

Even the taxi driver was grinning. I couldn't believe it when he lit up a cigarette himself, his eyes turning for a moment to look at me as he flicked his cigarette at another driver.

'So how did you cope with it?'

'I looked it up in some stupid book. How long it takes for the skin to regrow completely.'

'You did that? You went to the trouble of looking it up in a book?'

'Yeah.'

'And how long did you find it takes the whole skin to regrow?'

'Seven years, I estimated.' Seven years in fact not just for your skin but for every cell in your body. I was that jealous it had to be every cell in your body. Every cell except those in the brain, because they never tick over. They stay hard-wired. So your mind never forgets the delight of being kissed all over.

'Seven years!' chortled Harry. A hesitation, sniffing the tears of laughter back up into his nose, putting his thoughts in order. 'So how did she do it? How did she dump you?'

'Go to hell!' I say.

My fists are clenched but I know that I will tell him, when the anger settles. I might as well tell him now. It is a thing that has to come out. As Harry's war needed to come out.

'We went on holiday together. It was soon after she got the results of her A-levels and she knew she had the grades she needed for university. We went for a week's holiday to Majorca. Neither of us had ever been there before. We had never been on holiday together before.

'We stayed in one of the usual places: a made-up holiday village, built out of whitewashed concrete on a bay of the sea. It was blisteringly hot but you could go up on to these dunes out of the village and swim or snorkel. There was a restaurant under a canopy where the tables and chairs were stuck into the sand. You could get as blasted as you like and just bake in the sun.'

'There was something else you could do.'

'Yeah. But you got tired even of that after three or four days. So we decided to hire a four-wheel drive. It had an open top and you were about six feet off the ground. It cost a bomb and we could hardly afford it. Anyway, I drove us around the island. It was pretty sound, tearing around these roads into the mountains, where there was such a drop she was screaming and tugging on my arm.

'It was only in the last two days we found this really out-of-the-way place. A real Spanish place, where the old women wore black clothes and wide-brimmed straw hats. It was a small fishing village that was falling down in places and they were just laying the first tarmac over what were mostly dirt streets. Then we drove out of the town and along another dirt road. There were clouds of dust following us. That was where we found the little beach, with a turquoise sea, opposite the last bar in civilisation. It was something Tabi said, when we were stepping down straight on to the hot sand of the beach...

'"It's Paradise, Mylie!" That was what she said, her exact words.

'There were just a few elderly naturists, who had found the beach before us. We had to hide our faces we were laughing so much.

'We had a swim in the bay and then we lay back on the sand and let the sun dry us off. Then we went and shared a big plate of chips. We washed it down with two pints of beer in the bar, on tables made out of planks under a thatched roof. We liked it so much, the place and the beer, that we had two more pints to drink. That was how we spent all of the afternoon, drinking beer and just looking out on to Paradise. Later in the afternoon, after the nudists had gone, we managed to find ourselves a spot. That was when I sensed it for the first time. It was a feeling, like a terrible sadness, that was coming between us.'

Like at the end of *Truly, Madly, Deeply*.

I was silent now, and so was Harry, realising he had gone too far. He was his old understanding self again, allowing me a few moments of silence.

'Afterwards, we were just sitting there, waiting to see the sun setting over the sea. There was only one of the nudists left, a fat man with a white bum that made us laugh, fishing off the rocks at the end of the beach. You could actually see the sun go down. It wasn't really red, more of an orange – like a big orange ball. It changed shape. It became an oval and then it grew rings around it, like the planet Saturn, as it sank within a minute or two down into the sea.

I remember feeling a bit shocked sitting there after the sun had gone down. I didn't know what to say. I remember there was a black blob of tar that had somehow got on to on my naked shoulder. I was scratching at it with my nail, trying to get rid of it.

I said to Harry, 'I can't remember any actual words. It was just a feeling. I worked it out for myself that Tabi had already decided she was going to leave me.'

Suddenly, it seemed, we were arriving out in front of Victoria Station. Awkward Harry had recovered his ability to walk. He climbed out of the taxi without needing any assistance and he stood by me on the pavement, after I had paid off the grinning driver.

'I didn't understand, Harry. She never really explained it to me in a way that made me understand.' I felt so wound up I was just staring around me out into the streets, not knowing what to say.

'She must have said something. What did she actually say? How did she break it off with you?'

I had Harry's pinstripe jacket over my arm as I was directing him towards the station entrance.

'She never told me to my face. She just left me a letter.'

It reminds me now to look for a convenient post box so I can send my own letter of explanation to Michael, posted first class, so he will get it when he arrives at work tomorrow morning.

So it has begun. We are moving out, a part of the two opposing streams of people, flowing through each other's currents, in and out of the estuary of Victoria Station. I can see how the recognition is shining in Harry's eyes. We buy the tickets and wait another thirty minutes at the Victoria Tavern, within the station. Here, we sit in the noise and bustle, with my big grey back pack, with the sleeping bags, rescued from the left luggage office and now between my ankles. I allow enough time for Harry to settle before I feel ready to explain the real purpose of coming here.

'I've taken you out, Harry, just for one day. That's all. It isn't a joke. It's a serious business. You could regard it as a kind of recreational therapy, if you like. But then you're going to have to go back to the Unit.'

'My goodness!' he laughs. 'I'm amazed that you've gone to so much trouble just for me.'

'So you don't mind? You'll be willing to take part in what I am planning to do?'

'Right now, I'd do anything for a bottle of brandy and a packet of King Edward Imperial cigars!'

I am forced to laugh but I am shaking my head.

'You have to enter into the spirit of it, Harry,' I admonish him. 'Otherwise, it just becomes a day at the seaside.'

'A day at the seaside with a friend!' he corrects me, smiling.

I have to reassure myself that it will take time. I must be patient, get the circumstances right and then, little by little, even Harry will discover the spirit of it. Meanwhile there is time for one more round of beers, and for Harry to pay a visit to the lavatories, where I have to pay twenty pence for him to go and empty his bladder.

While I am waiting for his return, I recall that final letter from Tabi. I still remember it perfectly, word for word, as we start to shuffle our assorted bags and baggage into a portable order, getting ready for platform 17 and the Brighton train.

> *Dear Mylie,*
> *There's nothing terrible, no big deal. You were the first for me. It was really great, the greatest experience in the world. But I haven't even got to know anybody else except you. And I am only eighteen years old. I feel very bad about this and I worry like mad that I am making this really big mistake. It could be just a temporary thing, although I know you would never forgive me anyway, so I am not trying to play around with you or anything. But I feel I want to experience new things. I feel I just have to get my space. It got too much. It was like claustrophobia or something for me in the end. I am truly, madly deeply sorry, Mylie. I will always love you in my way.*

28

So, you see, Harry, this is the route we have taken. This is how we have ended up here on the beach at Brighton. Even the drinking you might regard as an integral part of it. But it's okay. We are getting there by degrees, arriving at some level of mutual understanding.

Each of us has accepted his specific responsibility. I will maintain the fire, which I have built up with a neat pile of paper and driftwood. Meanwhile you will take charge of the cigars and brandy I bought for you back at the station. So you see, we are doing things according to the letter: whatever letter it is that instructs us to treat it with the proper gravitas, as we sit around our places by the fire. Not that it matters to you, Harry, since you are already set into your cynical smile. It is enough that you are here, the young man in the old man's face, the war-weary soldier inside the work-study engineer, with the face that everybody trusted.

Some time later, as we are just sitting on the beach and Harry is lighting up the second of his cigars, he turns and he says to me, 'You never talk about your mother. Don't you get along with her?'

'Oh, Mum and I are very close, even though we like to argue. Maybe we're too much alike. What my father had as a fighter, my mother has in stubbornness. She's the most stubborn person you have ever met.' I can't help but laugh now, talking to Harry about my mother, Brenda. 'We had to manage without my father, so we were always short of money. Mum would really drive me nuts at times, because of the tricks she got up to so she could save a little money. You wouldn't believe the lengths she would go to. Arguing with the butcher, or the girl at the supermarket counter. She'd go back and fight it out for a penny.'

I pause, smiling, remembering.

I look over at Harry, noticing the fact he is now glad to be wearing the jacket over the pullover. He is looking a little pale and drawn, holding out the packet of cigars in my direction. Unthinkingly, I accept a cigar, although I am not a cigar kind of person. I light it off a splinter of wood from the fire, take my first puff, inhale it deep, let it do its damage down there in my lungs, from where the nicotine circulation time to my brain is mere seconds. I wait for those seconds. Feel the hit.

I realise, after a minute or so that we have both fallen silent. But we are not uncomfortable with each other's silence.

I have never been to Brighton before so it has come as quite a surprise to me that it is not a beach of sand. It is a beach of small round pebbles you can pick up and hold, like a clutch of bird's eggs, in your hand. Nearby is a broken down hulk of a pier running into the sea, and at the top of the beach, now dusk is falling, there are brightly-lit arches selling the usual holiday stuff, and on the road at the top one or two nightclubs.

I have to admit that it both surprises and wounds me, Harry, when you return to the subject of me and Tabi.

You say, suddenly, out of the blue, 'She decided she had to act selfishly. For her own sake. She had her own life to live.'

I say nothing for a moment or two, blinking in surprise, aware of the rise of tension around the fire. I glance at you, Harry, where you are sitting in the shadows, with the play of the flames about your face. Your voice is very soft. Muted. A husky whisper, as if from a distance. It is carried away on the breeze that is itself as high-pitched as the cry of a gull, this breeze that is combing my hair. 'Let it go, Harry!' I remonstrate, quietly.

'She was afraid, Mylie. You have to think what is at stake here. Commitment for life. Of course she was afraid. We all are, when it comes down to it.'

'But she had time to think about things. And she never made contact all this time. Never even tried.'

'Perhaps even that was understandable.'

Understandable? I gaze out, into the falling night, in the direction of the sea, reflecting on those first few weeks of grief, after Tabi ended it. I take my first swig of Harry's brandy, a big gulp straight from the neck of the bottle. A lot of ideas, hardly any of them sensible, went through my mind in those awful weeks.

'What are you trying to say?'

'We don't always behave logically. A lot of the time we don't behave logically at all.'

'I don't understand.'

Harry looks at me directly a moment. 'I'm not sure you're being altogether logical yourself in bringing me here. You're going to end up in trouble.'

I realise that he must be cold and tired so I unroll one of the two sleeping bags. But Harry isn't interested in sleep for the moment. I say nothing, because that familiar spasm of anxiety strikes home in my gut. I had, in fact, thought a lot in recent days about what I was going to say at this point.

'It's really important, Harry. That's why I brought you here. I want you to try to take a step back from your worries, look around you and see for yourself that life goes on. Will you try to do that for me?'

It is Harry's turn to be silent. I can see that he is thinking about this, turning things over in his mind. I give him plenty of time, although I am wondering what he is really concluding. I am hoping he will accept my advice.

When, after many minutes, he does speak, his voice is calmly factual. 'Perhaps it wasn't just you she was running from.'

I notice, of course, that Harry has changed the subject. 'How do you mean, not just me?'

'Think about it, logically.'

I am trying to think about it.

I am remembering the embarrassing way I behaved. How I threw away the last straw of our relationship when Tabi hinted we could remain friends. But the passion was too deep for that. And then I've been hearing things from time to time, from my friends back in Sheffield. They have told me how Tabi has cut her hair short, how she has grown tense with people, stressed out by the first year of her course, the medieval stuff, from Chaucer to Shakespeare. I know all this. She talked about how she was dreading this year even when we were on holiday together. So any contact now, any new adventure into friendship, would bring me face to face with that. It would cheapen the memories. And the memories are all I have to keep.

'Has she taken up with somebody else?'

'I don't know for certain, but I don't think so.'

Harry smiles, shaking his head. 'When, exactly, did she give you the bad news?'

'I've already told you. After the holiday.'

'But what was it that went so badly wrong on the holiday?'

'I told you, Harry. Jesus, weren't you even listening to me?'

But nothing I say is capable of offending Harry. Not now, when he is downing a liberal brandy himself, then smoking his cigar lying back, deep in the shadows.

He murmurs, 'You'd like to think that if you had your time all over again you'd behave differently. But maybe the Hindus are right and it's all laid out for us. Though I wish I could undo some of the foolish things I have done.'

'Hey, you and me both!'

Harry smiles, then mops at his brow with his hand. I can't help noticing that he is sweating a lot. 'How did you afford it – the holiday?'

He is changing the subject again.

'Tabi paid for it.'

'A student?'

'Well – her father.'

Harry is struggling to sit up again. He makes a joke of his difficulty, puffing out his cheeks and tapping his chest.

But then, with shock, I understand what he is trying to tell me. It is only now that I realize what he means. Tabi's father must have played more of a part in it than I realised back then.

I sit still for a while and think about Doctor Stanley Mather, a tall, heavy-set man, who makes jokes about his fat belly in medical terminology. What was left of his hair was so grey it was impossible to work out if it had once been chestnut like his daughter's. Whenever I saw him he was wearing a baggy anorak with a fake fur hood, or a shirt on which that he hadn't bothered to fasten the sleeves, or a thick-knit pullover over wrinkled trousers. He never ironed his trousers, or anything else for that matter. He wore trainers or sandals, never shoes.

'People called him sarcastic,' I say. 'Because he barked at his patients, like a dog.'

Barked at people because he was unhappy for some reason? Of course I always knew that Tabi's father had paid for the holiday. But I never thought it was for the reasons that Harry is suggesting.

I am rubbing distractedly at my own brow. 'When I got to know Tabi's dad better, I thought he was probably shy. I found him easy to talk to. I could talk to him about anything.'

Like the Blues Giants, Lightnin Hopkins, John Lee Hooker and Muddy Waters. Or the way artists like Howlin Wolf made it possible for somebody like Captain Beefheart and his Magic Band to emerge and show the world the road to freedom.

'You liked him, didn't you?'

'I thought old Doctor Mather had a soft spot for me. I'm sure about it really, because he turned a blind eye to so much that Tabi and I got up to.'

'You were eighteen years old. In love. You couldn't see what was happening. She was his only daughter. He had lost his wife. He knew that one day Tabi would leave him. He could live with that. That was a hurdle in the future. But there was such intensity to you, to your relationship with his daughter, it must have threatened him here and now. He must have been feeling it already, every time he saw the two of you together - what it would be like to be left alone.'

'No, it wasn't her father. I did it, Harry. I did it, with my jealousy. My possessiveness.'

'You think that little fit of jealousy would offend a woman?'

I can't see his face, but I know that through his own pain, my friend Harry is smiling. How is it that you can share the pain of a friend through smiling?

'What are you saying?'

'She'd have laughed at you. She'd have treasured that jealousy from a lover. That jealousy would have only confirmed your love for her.'

I can't help the fact that my head inclines to one side, from the simple pain of the memory. I say nothing, just shake my head.

Harry closes his eyes for a moment. 'He was getting older. Feeling increasingly alone. You had your whole life to look forward to. He'd have weighed one thing against another. As you say, he liked you. But possession is a selfish thing.'

I look at Harry, who is wiping his brow with a paper towel. He has moved back so he is half reclining, the lower half of his body tucked down in the sleeping bag. I can hear the rustling as he continues to wipe his whole face with the towel. I am lying back myself on the pebbles, shivering a little while listening to the sounds of the breeze and the sea, behind the sounds of Harry wiping his face. To be honest with you, I don't like the fact he's sweating so heavily. I wonder what's really going on here.

I think about his diabetes. But I have already given him his evening medication, the correct dose, which he has swallowed down with a swig of brandy. There should be no problem. Then Harry does something out of character. He reaches out and he clasps my hand.

There is something awkward in his action, a telling clumsiness in that brief, fierce contact.

'Hey, are you okay?'

I hear a struggle, a new kind of breathlessness as he drops his head and gives up trying to find the words.

'Oh, Jesus, Harry!'

For a while I don't know what I am thinking. I hardly dare to think at all. I just sit on the beach frozen with shock, taking one swig after another of Harry's brandy, with the breeze on my face and the sea in my mind, until the bottle is long empty and discarded.

I have to close my eyes to stop the spinning, later on in the dark of night, when I come back to awareness. I find myself recalling the program on Channel 4 that captured my imagination. I can see them now really vividly, those spiders living in the riverbank in Australia, who climbed up the reeds to live in the clouds.

Waiting. I am still half dreaming, waiting in my dream for the moment when I shall really wake up again. In my head there is such a wonderful sense of peace, a feeling of communication so profound.

You see, I think I know now what Harry was thinking in those last few moments. I can understand the fact that there comes a time when it is just too much. There was a woman who came into the unit suffering from depression after the death of her husband. She just died of grief. People do that when they have had enough. They just decide for themselves that this is the moment when the clockwork stops: the clockwork that keeps us ticking over, that makes our hearts beat on from moment to moment, our lungs breathe, our minds reflect. Maybe that is what the whole thing is about. Maybe that is all there is to it, the fundamental truth of it.

And so you know, Harry, what is happening now. You know, as I know, that the ghosts are coming. They are gathering about me here on the beach: your departed ghost and the living ghosts of my Uncle Tony and my mother Brenda, just as they would gather around me when I was very small and I had got myself into trouble.

I cannot resist the compulsion to touch him, to kneel down and brush my fingers against the cold right hand that he kept out of the sleeping bag to put under his head, and which has broken free to trail across his chest. Then his face - I brush his face down his left cheek before I have to leave him lying there, with his eyes open.

I gaze down at him one last time as I climb to my feet, rubbing the pain of the pebbles from my knees. I just cannot bring myself to close his eyes. I leave his eyes open, by the embers of the fire, as I stumble down the pebbly beach.

And so I begin to tell my story. I tell it to you, to your spirit, Harry, starting with how, as a very young child, I fell in love with the sea. But you know how it is with me, I have to correct myself, because even as a kid love had to be an obsession.

Tonight, once more, I feel the irresistible pull of that compulsive need, as I walk towards the distant waves, where the sea is so low it lies truly at my feet. You wouldn't believe the way the night sky has expanded until it fills the whole of my vision. I am walking towards the great constellation of Orion the Hunter, frozen for eternity in his cave of charcoal-green. As I move still further out, leaving behind the light pollution, even as the dusting of the milky way appears, it seems to loom ever closer as I walk, the starry landscape becoming three dimensional, so that I only have to keep on walking and I'll be amongst them.

Yeah, Harry, I hear you chuckling – in ten small light years!

What you said, Harry – you hit that nail right on the head. I'm in trouble. There are going to be questions to answer in the difficult days that lie ahead. At the very least I'll be joining the ranks of the unemployed at The Palace and saying goodbye to my lovely Marantz CD-63 MKII KI Signature, and Tannoy Profile speakers.

That's just something I'm going to have to grin and bear. But there's compensation, as I now see it, something fine and simple I have learnt from you, Harry. I think it's all down to one thing: listening to what people have to say. I mean really listening, listening beyond the words, deep listening, the way you have to listen when somebody you care about is finding it hard to do the communicating.

I realise now that all the while I thought I was taking care of you, you were actually taking care of me.

You see, I've been thinking about what you said, about how Tabi's father was possessive, so, I'm thinking I owe it to you to cross the city to the Queen Mary and Westfield College and do some listening of my own. The way I see it now, what have I got to lose?

'Yeah!' I murmur, once more finding myself attempting to move my legs, only to end up shaking my head, all the while laughing the ghost of a laugh through my chattering teeth. All that time in the ocean and I didn't notice its passage. But now I find myself standing in the shifting surf, my legs so numb I am paralysed by the cold, stuck here between the two immensities of land and sea. I am aware only of the ghostly figures that have accompanied me here, who stand in the lapping waves beside me.

It is time for my mother to begin the interrogation. The way, as a kid, I would imagine it all before it actually happened.

'What happened, Mylie?'

I say nothing, as always.

In my mind I have switched on to Corinne Bailey Rae, the way I do that when I find I need to. Did you know, she comes from Yorkshire, just like me. She co-writes her own songs, which is a big plus in my pantheon. She was racially abused on a regular basis while growing up, for no reason other than the fact her skin is a mellow shade of brown, the inheritance of her father, who came from the island of St Kitts, her skin blended to *café au lait* through marriage to her Yorkshire mother. An interesting ethnic hybrid, just like me!

So what do you know – a new day dawning. Already I can hear the occasional car passing by along the road above. Time to get out – I know. That common sense need is cutting through the confusion of my senses: the real world closing in around me in the startle of new voices on the beach. As I wait for rescue, I am floating on this gentle cloud of silvery light that makes one of the sea and the sky.

It's comforting to hear Corinne's hurt-voice rendering of *Like a Star*. To tell you the truth, Harry, it's kind of enchanting – like making contact soul-to-soul with a new star being born.